LENA TAKES A FOAL

ONCE UPON A VET SCHOOL: VET SCHOOL 24/7

LIZZI TREMAYNE

Lizzi Tremayne / Blue Mist Publishing

Franklin Road, RD 2

Waihi, New Zealand 3682

www.lizzitremayne.com

Publisher's Note: This is a work of fiction. Names, characters, places, and incidents are a product of the author's imagination. Locales and public names are sometimes used for atmospheric purposes. Any resemblance to actual people, living or dead, or to businesses, companies, events, institutions, or locales is completely coincidental.

Formatting, cover design, artwork, and cover photos by Lizzi Tremayne

Cover photo by Fabrizio Verrecchia on Unsplash

Author photo by Kajai Lang PhotosByKajai@gmail.com

Previously published with Authors of Main Street in Anthology: Christmas Babies on Main Street 2017

From the **Vet School 24/7** sequence of the **Once Upon a Vet School** series

Lena Takes a Foal / Lizzi Tremayne 1st Edition December 2017

Printed in New Zealand and the United States of America

Draft2Digital Paperback Edition 2019 06 13-V19

ISBN 978-0-9941431-9-8

DEDICATED TO

the special horses in my life who have taught me so much:
Lady, Sunshine, and Milly

Sunny

Sky High

Jules (My Friend Julie)

Charro (So Far Charrolero)

Mickey (yep, same horse, same manners)

Mingo

Boulder (J.O.'s Surprise)

Goody (Living Word)

Cache (Surprise Cache)

Minty (The Quilter)

Strawberry

Toya (Blue Mist Montoya) and Maya (Blue Mist Shemaya)

and

Bailey

Most of you, probably all of you but Maya, are past the rainbow bridge in green pastures far, far away, but you're always in my heart.

With you, I could fly and be free. Upon your backs, you offered me control of my own world, and I thank every one of you from the bottom of my heart.

With all my love, forever

L-

CONTENTS

BOOKS BY LIZZI TREMAYNE

The Long Trails Series
A Long Trail Rolling (Book One)
The Hills of Gold Unchanging (Book Two)
A Sea of Green Unfolding (Book Three)

Multi-Series Samplers
Lizzi Tremayne First Chapter Sampler

The *Once Upon a Vet School* Series
~Vet School 24/7~
Fifty Miles at a Breath
Lena Takes a Foal
~Practice Time~
Greener Pastures Calling

Boxed sets with Authors of Main Street
Christmas Babies on Main Street
Summer Romance on Main Street
Christmas Wishes on Main Street

Boxed sets with Bluestocking Belles
Follow Your Star Home

*Sign up for Lizzi's VIP Club to hear about new releases and specials,
plus get your free sampler gift here:*

www.lizzitremayne.com/VIPFoal/

PRAISE FOR LIZZI TREMAYNE

With her debut novel, A Long Trail Rolling, *Lizzi was:*

Winner 2016 True West Magazine
Best Western Romance
Winner 2015 RWNZ Koru Award
Finalist 2015 Best Indie Book Award
Winner 2014 RWNZ Pacific Hearts Award
Finalist 2013 RWNZ Great Beginnings

"vivid, light and fast-paced... a ripping good read. "
—Deborah Challinor, number one bestselling author and historian

"An authentic, emotional story of one woman's fight for survival in an unforgiving landscape."
—Leeanna Morgan, USA Today bestselling author

"An impressive debut...a romance, a western, and an adventure story, all rolled up into a compelling read."
—Booksellers NZ

The Hills of Gold Unchanging:
"The pace is fast, there's plenty of action and adventure and a few twists I didn't see coming. Good characters plus excellent history equals a great read."
—Deborah Challinor, number one bestselling author and historian

"...superb storytelling."
—Judy Knighton, editor

"I particularly liked the attention to historical detail. This is an author who does her homework, and it shows... a cracking good yarn."
—Shelagh Merlin, NetGalley Reviewer

A Sea of Green Unfolding:
"the historical research is excellent...well-integrated into the narrative."
—Deborah Challinor, number one bestselling author and historian

"A lovely combination of historical accuracy and adventure... [a] beautifully researched and engrossing story."
—Shelagh Merlin, NetGalley reviewer

"Loved this book. The characters draw you in on a story filled with interest and suspense."
—Kate Le Petit

Fifty Miles at a Breath
"Lizzi Tremayne is a born storyteller. The...characters... [are] three dimensional and you can feel Lena and Blake's emotions."
—Lori Dykes

"a wonderful series about the path to becoming a veterinarian, the love of horses and sweet romance. Lena and Blake will grab your heart."
  −*Teri Donaldson*

Lena Takes a Foal

"This book is for anyone with a passion for horses… or anyone who loves a story about strong, independent young women finding love!"
  −*Stacey*

"The story… displays Lizzi Tremayne's ability to develop strong characters… with a nice strong black moment to challenge our heroine and prove her worth."
  −*Shelagh Merlin, NetGalley Reviewer*

"…the perfect blend of sweet romance, horses and real emotions with fascinating information woven in about the medical care of horses."
  −*Teri Donaldson*

"As I turned the last page I cannot stop smiling! I look forward to more in this series and from this author!!!"
  −*Lori Dykes*

1

Northern California, 1986

MICKEY'S ROAN EARS, silhouetted against the pale green light filtering into the tiny glade, rose higher and higher before me and my heart froze—he'd never reared this high before. The light disappeared as the horse's massive body blocked out the sun. A blinding flash of pain, and the scent of rotting leaves as my body hit the forest litter, then only blessed darkness.

SOMEONE WAS THERE in the darkness before us. Biting my lip, I reined Mickey to a halt at the sight of a strange white pickup truck. It glowed in the light of the dim bulb above the stable yard. The barn door creaked as it swung open, then closed behind the figure of a tall man. There weren't any men boarding horses here.

Who...?

I swallowed hard, glancing from side to side to see if anyone else was around, my fingers tightening on the reins. Mickey backed up a step, his bit clanking as he threw his head, and I gritted my teeth to keep from crying out with pain at the motion. The figure turned to face us.

"Hello, who's there?" he called out.

Kit Allen, a surgery resident from the veterinary school. I let out my breath and shivered as the butterflies dancing in my stomach nearly overcame even the throbbing in my leg.

"It's me, Lena Scott," I said.

He walked toward me and I squeezed my legs to move my horse forward before I thought. I yelped, but bit it off.

"What the heck are you doing out riding at this hour?" His brows narrowed as I rode up to him. "And what have you done to your face?"

"Ahhh... we had a... disagreement about going home."

"Looks like the roan won. Bit late for a ride, isn't it?" He set down a bucket full of bandaging materials and reached for one of Mickey's reins.

"I left mid-afternoon." I said, wincing. "I only got as far as the glade, a few miles across the fields."

"Are you okay?" He frowned as his eyes scanned the perfectly cool horse, then his gaze snapped to mine.

"I've hurt my leg." My attempt at nonchalance came out as a whine. My left foot hung free of the stirrup—the leg hurt too much to do anything else.

"What have you done with Lena?" Kit muttered, as he moved to the horse's near side and froze. He stared at the swelling bulging above the top of my boot, all the way to mid-thigh, then at my eyes, as comprehension dawned. "Is this horse named Mickey? What happened?"

I took a deep breath. I didn't want anyone to know, especially someone from the vet school.

"Yes, it's Mickey. He fell on me."

"He fell? It's flat out there." His voice was terse and the furrows on his brow deepened.

"He went over backwards," I whispered, my heart in my throat.

"That riding school he came from—" He stopped and gritted his teeth. "Anyway, you're hurt," he said, his voice softening. "Can you get down?"

I shook my head.

"I was wondering how I'd get off," I said, surveying the rickety old corral fences.

"Let me help." He was tall enough to hold me around the waist and pull me carefully from the saddle, while I sternly told the butterflies to go to play somewhere else. I clamped my jaws together when I my bad limb bumped against his, but I couldn't help gasping when it hit the dirt.

"I'll put the horse away and give you a ride," Kit said, and released me as soon as I could bear weight on it.

"I can drive mys—"

"—good thing you were wearing that thing. There's a great dent in it." He raised a brow at me, eyeing the back of my helmet. "You were knocked out, weren't you?"

I closed my eyes and took a deep breath. "I don't know."

"Right. I don't know what you had planned, but you won't manage the heavy clutch in your old truck with that leg, will you?"

"I hadn't actually thought past getting back to the barn in one piece," I mumbled, mostly to myself, as he led the horse away. I wrung my hands. "His feed's made up," I called after him.

"I'll find it." Kit slipped the girth as he walked and pulled the saddle off.

I limped to get my backpack, then leaned against Kit's truck and closed my eyes. The sweet scent of an early-blooming honeysuckle wafted to me on the breeze, as I cooled the burning abrasions on the back of my arms against the vehicle's metal panel. Maybe I should press my hot cheeks against it, and the rest of my aching body. A wry grin formed on my lips.

I started when Kit spoke.

"Hop into the truck," he called, from inside the barn, as he led the roan into his stall. Kit growled something low at the horse, then exited the barn with my saddle over his arm.

"Can't you get in?" he said, as he walked up.

I shook my head and glanced down at my swollen leg.

His eyes following mine, he grimaced, picked me up with care, and set me on the passenger seat. At the sight of the forms and equipment filling the middle of the bench seat, I recognized the truck. It belonged to the clinics at the vet school.

"We need to get that boot off and get you to the hospital," he said.

"I'll be fine at home, thanks."

"You need the hospital." His brows narrowed until they nearly touched.

"No. Thank you."

He quirked his lips in silence for a moment. "How about student health?"

"I'll be fine. They'll tell me to elevate it, take anti-inflammatories, and rest."

"Yes, but you could have more injuries than you realize."

"Can you please look at my leg for me?"

"Your leg's a mess, but it's your head that worries me." He sighed and pulled a penlight from his pocket, flicked it at my eyes, first one, then the other, then back and forth between them several times.

"Your light reflexes are normal, but that leg…"

"It'll be fine. I've had worse."

He squeezed his eyes shut for a moment.

"Home it is, then, but get it checked out tomorrow, okay?"

Every tiny bump in the road on the way home jarred my leg. By the time we got near home, I was nearly vomiting from the pain, but riding beside Dr. Kit Allen made up for a lot. For the past few years, he'd had my utter admiration—bordering on hero worship—though he didn't know me from a bar of soap. He was a magician with horses and really cared about them—not just their diagnosis and treatment—but *them*. I glanced across the cab to his profile, outlined by a streetlamp. Pretty drop-dead gorgeous, too, if you happen to like your classical tall, dark and handsome. But his way with horses— that really got to me.

I shook my head.

Just remember how tall, dark, and handsome turned out last time.

"Is there someone at your place who can help you with your boot? Getting it on—off, I mean?" He flushed in the glow from the dashboard lights and clamped his lips together.

I clamped my own to keep from grinning at his blush. Made me feel better about mine, but it wasn't helping me keep my mind where it belonged, really.

Residents didn't usually consort with students, and I'd never spent time around him, other than reporting on his cases in ICU... and watching him when he wasn't looking. He had a sharp wit, but he didn't say much, and hailed from the snobbiest horsey town in our home county, so I'd kept my distance, despite his regular appearances in my dreams for the past several months. Maybe he was just shy. He'd been pretty nice tonight—the butterflies started kicking again, and I told them to quit.

"My housemate Tamarah might be home," I finally answered.

He let out a long breath and a hint of a smile touched his lips.

"You might get that field boot off before some idiot wants to cut it off...the *only* reason not go to the hospital, I guess," he said, with the hint of a grin.

"Call me vain," I said, as I reached down to loosen its lace, with a sharp inhalation at the stabbing pain in my ribs "but I'd almost rather cut off my leg than this Dehner boot—I've waited two decades to own a pair... you'd understand about good boots."

"How's that?"

"Some comment I overheard in ICU, sorry," my cheeks heated further, "about you showing hunter-jumpers—to the degree of resetting shoes between judges to change your horses' movement."

"We were kinda serious." He grinned. "Good thing I worked my way through college as a farrier. Kept the bills down."

No lights showed from the windows as we stopped before my house. This time he didn't even ask if I could manage. He came around to my side, picked me up and carried me to the door as if weighed nothing. Desired or not, having his face that up-close and personal was disconcerting, so I turned my heated cheeks away and fumbled with the house keys as we stood exposed in the light of the bare porch bulb.

Ten minutes later, nauseous, with more swearing and tears than I'd have preferred, we got the boot off, intact.

"There's a bandage in the bathroom, top drawer, and naproxen in the cabinet," I said, as the room swam a bit with the pain and the sight of my leg, already blue from toes to groin.

"Are these yours?" He shot me a look and held up my skimpy running shorts. My face must've gone from white to red, now. The scrap of nylon had been on the bathroom floor beneath some even scantier lacy panties.

I somehow nodded. He tossed the shorts to me and disappeared.

"Put them on, please," he called from the bathroom. "I'd like to check that leg."

Sounded like he was talking about a horse. I grinned, despite myself, and managed to peel my breeches down and off, then tugged the shorts up as he returned with a compression bandage, pills and a glass of water.

Dr. Allen blinked at the leg, shaking his head, then checked the femur, tibia and fibula for stability. Taking the heel in one hand, he flexed, extended, and rotated the joints in all directions, but nothing crunched, while I held myself rigid and bit the insides of my cheek till I tasted blood. It'd be the hospital for sure, if I let myself scream.

"No crepitus, and the joints work fine. I'll bandage it up, but you *must* get it looked at." He looked at me with suspicion. He must've known I had no intention of visiting the good doctors of the university health center.

I compressed my lips together. I had two weeks to recover before school and work started again.

Piece of cake.

$$\diagdown\!\!\!\!\triangleright$$

FOR ALL MY BRAVADO, Tamarah, my fourth-year vet student housemate, still had to go with a friend to the barn the next day to pick up my truck and feed the horse—I wasn't going anywhere.

"How did you get back?" Tamarah said, after she returned. "It's a long way to the barn from where he dumped you."

"Rode back," I mumbled through a full mouth.

"Didn't Mickey leave?"

"When I woke up in the dark, I still had his reins in a death-grip," I said. "I learned young to keep hold of my reins when I fell off—riding boots aren't exactly made for hiking home in the Santa Cruz Mountains."

"How'd you get back on him? That's your mounting leg." She frowned at my swollen appendage.

"Hopped to a fallen log, clinging to his mane, then clambered onto his back all anyhow, swearing and sweating like a demented thing. I still ache all over."

"And you haven't seen a doctor?" Tamarah said, glancing up from her granola.

"It's okay, Dr. Allen checked it out."

Tamarah blinked.

"Dr. Allen? The resident? Where did you see him?"

"He was at the barn when I rode in on Mickey."

"That's all very well," she set down her spoon down carefully, "but he's a vet. You need a human doctor."

"Are you serious, Tam?" I stared at her. "They'd put me in the hospital."

"Where you belong," she stated flatly.

"I can't make my rent if I don't finish typing Sarah Kennedy's doctoral dissertation before school starts again."

"You can do that in hospital."

"Yeah, I can't even lift my typewriter. I'm sure that'll work," I said, crossing my arms and leaning back with a yelp. I kept forgetting about my ribs. "I'll just have to take care of it at home. I can keep it elevated and massage the heck out of it."

She shook her head as she rinsed her bowl in the sink.

"Besides, if I'm in the hospital and miss classes, I'll never catch up."

"Of course, you will." Her brows narrowed at me. "Why didn't Dr. Allen take you to the hospital?"

"He tried," I said, wincing.

"Sometimes you have rocks in your head, girl." Tamarah shook her head as she picked up my bowl. She slapped it down on the counter and stalked off.

Some people just seem to be born brilliant. Like Tamarah. Somehow, I'd ended up with 150 of them in my vet school class. The rest of us work our buns off just to survive.

I'm not bitter, it's just the way it is.

THE JINGLE of the ice cream truck pulled me out of whatever internal medicine doctorate-dissertation trance I was in, typing myself stupid. I'd been stuck in bed with Sarah's *Previously Unknown E. coli in a Dog* for nearly a week and I had a desperate urge to catch that truck—and snag me a chocolate gelato.

Never mind I could barely make it to the toilet.

With a frown at Tamarah's makeshift desk sitting over my reclining body, topped by 35 pounds of IBM Selectric correcting typewriter, I bit my lip, held my breath and heaved. My sore ribs shrieked, but the typewriter barely budged. I tried again and managed to tip it off my lap, then swung my legs across and dived for the door... but my leg was trapped in the sheets, wasn't it?

I hit the floor with a grunt and a scream, then dragged myself to the door frame and climbed up its slippery surface.

That ice cream had better be good.

I staggered down the hallway, leaning against the wall as I went. If I'd gone to the doctor, I'd no doubt have a crutch, but my stupidity might cost me that gelato. I could almost taste it and I hurried, nearly falling over Tamarah's golden Labrador as she rushed up to me, leash in mouth and a hopeful look in her big brown eyes.

"Watch out, Susie, not now," I mumbled, then stumbled down the porch steps. I was limping across the lawn at a great rate of knots when the brightly painted van, playing its merry tune, drove away in a cloud of diesel smoke.

I growled beneath my breath at the universe for denying me the chance to add inches to my waistline, then took a deep breath. The mailbox stood just yards away. I might as well check it, now I was out here. As I reached into the box, a movement to my right caught my eye.

"Susie, what have you got?" I called out to the dog. She looked at me, all big, innocent Labrador eyes, a half-grown bunny draped through her mouth.

"Gently, gently," I whispered, as I picked up her forgotten leash and followed her into the bushes, dragging my screaming leg. A domestic rabbit like this baby Belgian Lop running around in the middle of town must be someone's pet. It was still alive, its little chest heaving in triple time, but that could change in a heartbeat.

"Come on, Susie, give it here," I cajoled, and waved the leash at her.

With a joyous look, she spat the rabbit at me and lunged for the leash. I dove for the bunny like a wide receiver making the final play in the end zone, quite forgetting for one brief moment that I only had one functional leg.

This time, I'm sure the whole neighborhood heard me swear.

Lucky Susie. She got her walk after all. We returned to the house to put the little hopper in a box with some water and lettuce to calm down while I fashioned a rough—operative word, rough—crutch. With the Labrador helping, against my wishes and better judgement, I loaded the bunny into a backpack. It snuggled down and never moved, as we set off to tour the neighborhood. I'm not sure if Susie's enthusiasm helped, but I hobbled from house to house, muttering a fairly constant stream of imprecations under my breath. It took over an hour to canvass the neighborhood, but we finally found a little old lady whose eyes watered up when I mentioned the rabbit. Her granddaughter brought it over to show it off last week—and forgot about it while it grazed on granny's back lawn. When they returned, of course it had gone walkabout. They thought they'd never see it again.

Made my day.

A FEW DAYS LATER, despite the hydrotherapy, massage, and loving care by Tamarah, the leg actually looked worse. Not content to stay a nice blue color, it had morphed to a purple, black and yellow camo pattern. Understanding the medical significance of the color changes was all very nice, but it sure didn't make the bruises resolve any faster.

"Do you want to see that blasted horse of yours?" Tamarah said the next day, out of the blue.

"Really? You'll take me?"

"I go there every day to take care of him, anyway." She scowled at me. "You might as well come along... on one condition."

"What is it?" I said, rather ungraciously, under the circumstances. She'd been caring for me, too, since my fall. I peered sideways at her.

"We go by student health on the way back. I don't want to come home from walking the dog to find you seizuring from a blood clot in your brain."

Susie jumped to her feet at the W-word and spat her slimy tennis ball at me. I sidestepped, with a yelp, but offered the dog a twisted grin. After the bunny incident, I had a new appreciation for her ability to hurl things with her mouth.

"My father would shoot me," Tamarah continued smoothly, "if he knew I'd let you stay away from the doctor."

That got me.

Tamarah's daddy, a lovely man, was also a professor... at our veterinary school. I bit my cheek. He wouldn't be impressed by my irresponsible behavior. Now was not the time to annoy his daughter. It has also occurred to my thick little brain that a more comfortable crutch could be useful when school started—a mere few days from now.

"Thanks," I managed, past gritted teeth. "I'd like that...the first part, but... I'll go to the doctor."

"Get a sock on that foot and we'll go," she said.

I hopped away as fast as I could, before she could change her mind.

It was sure good to be at the barn again. Swallows flitted in and out of the hay loft and blooming flowers combined with the smell of molasses to make me feel at home. Mickey at least had the decency to look guilty when I limped toward him with his feed. Afterward, while Tamarah cleaned his stall, I mooned over the fence at him, breathing in his newly-mown hay scent and running my fingers through his mane.

"Don't even think about taking him for a walk, much less riding." Tamarah stood between me and the tack room with a look on her face that made me cringe.

I quashed the desire to ask for his halter and kissed his soft nose, instead.

TAMARAH HELD open the front door of student health for me, with a triumphant smile.

Are you coming in?" I asked her.

"I'll just wait out here," she said. "I'm not so keen on going to the doctor, either."

I shook my head at her, with a wry grin. The disinfectant scent of hospital entered my nostrils and clung to the sides of my tongue as I walked to the receptionist.

"This didn't just happen," the doctor said, when my turn

to see her finally came. "You could have had clots! How long has it been?"

"A week and a half," I mumbled into my shirt.

"I see you rushed right in," she said, in a huff, and shook her head. "What have you been doing for this leg?" She gently prodded at the still-swollen tissue.

Her demeanor softened a little when I told her, but she still scowled.

"I guess you're out of the danger zone, anyway. I'd have hospitalized you."

I nodded.

"So you start school next week? What are you studying?"

"Vet med."

"Vet?" She blinked. "You should know bett—oh well, vet students... " she sighed, and shook her head again as she scribbled in her notes. "Never mind. Small animals, I hope? Try to stay off it. Sit down while you're treating your patients."

I mumbled something incoherent. I didn't have the heart to tell her I was Equine Track and worked as a Large Animal ICU Technician. Galloping on foot between three barns, running IV fluids to twelve horses at a time, and tubing colicky horses all night was standard. I couldn't tell her. She'd have the vapors.

Oblivious to her patient's dastardly plans, the doctor smiled and left me with a packet of anti-inflammatories and admonitions to rest, elevate it, and keep up the massage.

At least I could hold my head up in front of Tamarah again, but I was still glad school was about to start. While I appreciated her loving, if tight-lipped, care, I really didn't need the pillow under my leg fluffed every half hour. Worse, if I kept drinking so many hot chocolates, I'd never fit into my jeans again when the swelling in my leg eventually went down. My biggest worry now, though, was getting to class on time—

never one of my strong points, anyway—but doing it hopping would make it even more tricky.

My friend Jess returned from a trip away with her family the night before classes were to resume.

"Did you see what our first lecture is tomorrow?" Her voice leapt with expectancy over the phone line

I pulled the schedule from my bag, where it had lain, forgotten, since the final day of last quarter. One glance, and my grin at her excitement vanished. Spots swam before my eyes as I read the title of the first lecture:

Dystocia: Difficult Birth in the Mare. Determining the Need for Surgical Intervention

I nearly dropped the phone.
Not dystocia. Not foaling difficulties.
Anything but that.

2

———

I leaned against a wall in the foyer, resting after my struggle to get to the classroom. When I'd gotten my breath back, the mere thought of the upcoming session's topic made me start hyperventilating again... and the talk hadn't even started.

When the lecturer entered the anteroom, I closed my eyes for a moment, and my already-warm face heated some more. It wasn't Dr. Rye today, as scheduled, but Kit.

No—it's Dr. Allen, I reminded myself, because I needed to think of him that way again. He looked up and our eyes met.

"How's the leg?" he said, his cheeks flushing as he approached.

"It's fine, thanks." I ducked my head and tried to ignore the fist curling in my gut, then peered up at him.

He raised an eyebrow and glanced down at the crutch lodged in my armpit.

"So, you *did* see a doctor, after all?"

"Yes, and thanks for your help that night." I looked at the floor. "It would have been a long walk home."

"It could have been rough," he agreed.

I nodded while he hovered, as students flowed past us into the lecture hall. They flicked glances our way before walking down the steps toward their seats.

"Well, I'd best get prepared for my lecture." Kit hesitated, then frowned. "Are you okay? You're awfully pale."

"I've been behaving, staying inside with my leg up." I looked away, then glanced back to see his eyes narrow further.

"You take care of yourself, eh?"

"I promise." I risked a smile upward.

He motioned for me to precede him down the steps, then headed for the podium. His slide carousel clicked into place as I worked my way across the row of seats. I stowed the wooden crutch by my feet and sank down with a sigh of relief. It was a long hobble from the bus stop, but it beat walking or driving my beast of a pickup. It'd definitely be a while before I could ride my bicycle.

Jess bounced into the seat beside me and looked down at the floor.

"A crutch? Whose is that? Yours?"

"Nailed, first guess." I gave her a lopsided grin.

"What have you done now?"

I hesitated. She'd scream at me, class or no class.

"Slipped on some stairs and twisted my ankle. Sprained, doctor says."

"Seriously? Sprained on steps?"

I bit my lip.

"Welcome back to school, everyone," Kit called out, right on time.

Jess looked at me from the corners of her eyes while she pulled her notebook out, then turned her attention to the lecturer.

It seemed everything might just be all right. Kit, *no, Dr. Allen*, had plenty of cute slides of healthy mares and foals cavorting in grassy fields. He even got a grin out of me. I began to breathe again and shared a smile with Jess.

"That's when everything goes as planned," Dr. Allen's voice cut into my reverie and I gulped, "but this is a surgery lecture," he continued, "and I wouldn't be here speaking with you if everything always went right."

I gripped my hands together as they began to shake. "When everything goes to plan, most mares drop their foals within twenty to sixty minutes after their water breaks." He flicked slowly through the next few slides.

He proceeded, relentlessly—pre-and full-term mares, late ones—and finally, presentations of the fetus requiring veterinary intervention. My pen clattered onto the concrete as my world began to fragment.

Image after image of ropes attached to tiny legs protruding from beneath the tails of down, sweaty mares, and one with red—oh man, the red—coating the mare's backside, the veterinarian, and the straw. Gripping my armrests, I bit my lip until my own blood came, willing myself to hold on. I finally gave up, staggered sideways along the aisle, and raced for the back door. I barely made it to the women's locker room.

I wiped my face after my time spent kissing the commode and tried to rinse the foul taste from my mouth.

Hot, flushed cheeks and haunted, green eyes peeked from beneath my profusion of brown hair in the mirror. I bullied the mass into shape with my fingers and braided it down my back to my waist, then collapsed onto a bench, eyes squeezed shut against the tears threatening to escape.

I couldn't go back in there. How would I ever pass my Equine Surgery, much less my Equine Reproduction rotations? I wouldn't graduate, wouldn't practice, and would never finish what I set out to achieve at seven years of age. Most importantly, I couldn't ever pay the horses back what I owed to them.

I wanted to melt into the shiny pink and gray tiles on the floor and not have to face my classmates, Dr. Allen, or anyone else.

I JUMPED, with a shriek, as the door slammed back against the wall. Jess strode into the locker room, lugging both of our backpacks and my crutch.

"Are you okay?" Her concerned frown helped.

"A little better now," I said.

"Stomach bug?"

"Last night's chicken must've been bad."

"You missed a great lecture," she said, as a smile stretched wide across her face. "He talked all about cesareans, midline and standing flank—"

"—can we talk about it some other time?" I interrupted.

"Sure, I'm sorry. Are you well enough to make our next lab?"

"I'm sure I will be. Maybe I'll go over to *The Granary* and have a drink."

"Thought you'd never ask," Jess said. She held the door open as I stumbled out into the hallway—and nearly crashed into my last disaster.

Gareth Barnett-Payne dodged clear, his bedroom-brown eyes taking in my tear-stained face. He looked me up and down as I stood like a rabbit in the headlights, frozen. He flicked his dark mane back, smirked, turned on his heel, and continued down the hall, whistling beneath his breath.

"Glad you've done with *that* creep," Jess muttered, with a scowl at him. "Come on, we have better things to do than look at the likes of him."

I inhaled slowly and followed her. Kit, *Dr. Allen*, I nearly screamed at myself, caught up with us as we neared the front entryway.

"I didn't *think* you looked well," he said, with a frown. "Are you sure you should be up, with that leg?"

Jess glanced at me and I looked away.

"I'll go have a rest before my lab." I tried to smile at him, but I think it came out more like a wince. "Thanks for asking."

"Any time," Kit said, with his killer smile and a glint in his eye. He held the door of the building open for us before he turned back toward his office.

A few feet behind Jess, I gathered what was left of my wits while my gaze shifted back to the vet school's grand entrance. As I did every time upon entering or leaving the building's hallowed halls, I nodded a greeting to my old friends, the menagerie of raised-relief marble animals surrounding the doors. I'd first seen the beasties on a 4-H Club field trip as a pre-teen. They always reminded me why I was here... and that whatever effort it took to get here was completely and utterly worth it. I owed animals, especially horses, so much.

My heart a bit lighter, I limped on down the steps to catch my friend. Just down the block, beside the road teeming with students on bicycle and foot, the front door of *The Granary* stood open. I sighed in relief. Jess flicked a look back toward the vet school, then rounded on me.

"What does Dr. Allen know about your leg?"

"He-he saw me twist my ankle." I bit my lips together and stumbled as my bad leg gave way beneath me. I lost my balance and staggered sideways into the pannier of a passing bicycle.

"Sorry," called the bicyclist, as my world exploded.

Only years of working with green horses stopped me from shrieking as I sprawled face-first, willing the pavement to swallow me, while the blinding white pain in my leg blanked everything else out.

"Are you okay, Lena?" Jess's voice came from far away, as I hunched into a ball over my tucked-up leg. I didn't think it could bend that much. Go figure.

"I—I think so."

"You aren't okay." She ducked down beside me.

"Yeah, well, it's a bad sprain." I've never been able to lie to save myself. I struggled to a sitting position and blinked away the blurriness.

"Lena, you look like a ghost—*tears*? He didn't hit you that hard, what's up?"

I couldn't tell her. She'd warned me.

"And what's with the skirt and thigh-high boots? I've never seen you out of jeans."

Silence.

"Oh," she said, assessing. "Better question, why *aren't* you wearing jeans?"

"Can't," I mumbled to my pearl snaps. She'd find out soon enough anyway. I probably wouldn't be able to walk after this —the leg throbbed like it had on the first day.

"So, what's up, chick?"

I froze as she lifted the hem of my skirt and gasped.

"Let's go," I muttered. "I'm glad it's close. Don't think I could walk much further." Yep, it was worse now for sure.

Jess pulled me to my feet and I turned toward the smell of brewing coffee from our favorite haunt. Trying to think of anything but my screaming leg, I wondered how something that smelled as good as coffee could taste so bad. I wiped the sweat from my brow as Jess and I struggled up the coffeehouse's steps.

She dragged me to a corner booth and slid me onto the smooth seat.

"Put your leg up on that," she said. "Chocolate?"

"You're a godsend," I whispered, as she scurried off, then I bodily lifted my booted foot up onto the cushion. I thought

I'd need a scalpel to cut the silence after she returned. I looked up at her cute blonde curls peeking from beneath her cowboy hat and dropped my eyes again.

She sat in silence for a few minutes, then narrowed her brows and cut straight to the quick.

"It was that horse."

"Okay, I fell off," I murmured, looking away. I scrabbled in my bag for a pen, hoping she'd believe me, but knowing she wouldn't.

Her fingernails beat out a tattoo on the table top and I finally glanced up to her frown.

"Let's have a better look at that leg." Refusal wasn't an option, by the tone.

As my clammy fingers slowly pulled the skirt up to my groin and Jess pushed the boot down toward my nonexistent ankle, her complexion faded to a sort of gray. Heck, the leg looked better than it had a week ago, but I wasn't *about* to tell her that.

"Shit."

Uh-oh. Jess never swears.

"What did the doctor say?" She raised a brow at me. The steel in her baby blues warned me not to lie. "You *did* go, didn't you?"

"Yes." I'd have to remember to thank Tamarah. Without her insistence, Jess would be dragging me down the street toward student health right now.

"Why aren't you in the hospital? By the colors in that leg," Jess said, "it's been two weeks. Just when did you see this doctor?"

I stared into the depths of my mug for as long as I dared.

"Three days ago," I said, to the dregs of marshmallow and cocoa in the bottom.

"No time like the present, eh? Why'd you wait so long?

Death wish?" Jess was nearly shouting. "What, did Tamarah make you go?"

"You should thank me—you get to see pathology in action," I said lightly, but neither the full-color contusion demonstration nor my attempt at veterinary humor did the trick. I gulped.

"Why is it so hard to take care of yourself?" Jess said, shaking her head.

"You know why," I growled. "She'd have put me in the hospital. I can't just stop—"

"—oh, hell," she snarled, "you could have had a stroke and died."

"I'm still here." I shrugged, with a twisted grin. "Hard to kill a weed."

She closed her eyes and leaned over the table to hug me, carefully.

"But a much loved one, you idiot. Drink up, we need to move on soon—" she broke off and frowned, but seemed to reconsider. She drank her coffee, peering at me from the corners of her eyes occasionally, then we headed slowly back to lab at the teaching hospital barn, watching over our shoulders for more demon bicycles.

I'D HOPED Jess had been effectively distracted from the details of how my injury happened, but I should have known there was a reason she cooked dinner for me that night. Turned out it wasn't just pity after all. Fancy that. She waited in silence until I was cornered behind the little table in her student digs.

"Tell me," Jess said.

Knowing what was coming, I concentrated on slicing a piece of spaghetti into 0.25 cm lengths like a microtome, afraid to look up from the perfect sections.

"How you did that." She nodded at my leg.

"I told you." I squirmed. "I fell off."

"No, you didn't," she said, barely audible, and I jumped as her fork hit the table with a clatter. "The truth," she barked.

It never pays to mess around with a horsey girl.

Jess sat, waiting for an eternity, arms folded against her chest.

I took a deep breath.

"Mickey and I disagreed. I wanted to go on and he wasn't so keen."

"And?"

I took a deep breath. This *wouldn't* be pretty. "And he reared," I said, in a rush.

"And I suppose you fell off and knocked that leg on a branch, right?" she said, from between gritted teeth, as her eyes shot daggers. "How stupid do you think I am? That blasted nag threw himself over backwards and landed on you, didn't he?"

I couldn't even try for a reasonable excuse. Jess had known all along. Last year, she'd begged me not to buy the roan for that express reason.

"That horse'll be the death of you." She sat still, head in hands. "And this isn't the first time. He's been doing it for years at that riding school where you bought him," she said, when she finally looked up. "He knew the fastest way home from a ride on the levees was to back up to a deep, steep-sided irrigation ditch and rear."

"Yeah," I whispered, staring at my plate. "I saw him do it, once. That student took one look over her shoulder at the water in the bottom of the drain and practically let him gallop home. Never rode him again."

"So why did you think Mickey'd be any different for you?"

"We usually get along well. This was the first time he went that high with me."

"Yeah, well," Jess drew a big breath, "it might have been the last. Don't you get it?"

"Yeah, but what else can I do? As fantastic as he is in the arena and on the cross-country course, nobody else'll tolerate his behavior. He'd just end up in a can." I stirred swirls into the sauce on my plate, and the scent of garlic tickled my nose. "I can usually keep him in line—but I wasn't on my game that day and he hadn't had enough work lately. *Mea culpa.*"

She shook her head, then jerked it up and stared at me.

"So, what does Dr. Allen *really* know about it?"

I shredded my nails beneath the table while I my brain scrambled for an answer.

"He was at Mickey's stable when I rode in after my accident."

"And?"

"And, it was dark. No one was around. I had no idea how I was going to get off the horse, much less drive my truck—and there he was. My knight in shining armor, just coming out of the barn. He was... a lot kinder than I expected he'd be."

"Lucky you." She raised a brow. "Was it nice?"

"As nice as it *could* be, with my leg, ribs, and scraped up body throbbing all to hell."

"Miranda will be so jealous."

"Miranda?" I stared at her blankly.

"In our class. She's been tagging after him, but he seems to be running just a little faster than she is."

"He's a resident, and we're students," I said, flatly, then added, in my best snobby tone, "Not a gratuitous combination, by all accounts, according to the edicts handed down from the veterinary school hierarchy through perpetuity."

"That's never stopped you from looking at him before," she said, with a sly look at me.

"Yeah, well," I flushed so hot, my cheeks burned, "no use being a fly on the windshield...again. It's not going to happen. I'm sure I'll get over a little crush."

Jess gave me a twisted grin and chuckled. "We'll see," she said.

3

D r. Rye was our lecturer for Wednesday's Equine Surgery lecture, so I didn't have to see Ki—*Dr. Allen*, and my focus in class was impeccable.

It seemed I only had to think about Kit for my face to heat up—and it was starting to look like I had it bad. Maybe that's why I nearly dropped a half-full container of colostrum when his voice came from over my shoulder as I struggled to get into a comfortable position, half-kneeling, halfway underneath a mare in the Large Animal ICU stall.

"What the heck are you doing under there?" Kit growled.

"What does it look like? Milking a mare," I said, my voice shaky. It had taken the better part of a half hour to milk this much out of her, never mind having to do it in strange contortions around my non-bending limb.

"Does your supervisor know what your leg looks like?" He frowned.

That got my attention. I whipped my head around to see if my boss had heard him and nearly tipped over, then clambered the rest of the way to my feet.

"Please Ki—Dr. Allen, please don't say anything to Frank.

I need the hours—I can't feed that horse or me without it." I was pleading, now.

"You're a pain in the rear, you know?" Kit shook his head. "But you're a trier, I'll give you that. Hasn't anyone shown you how to milk a mare with a syringe?"

"A syringe? I think she might object." I had to grin at that. "She's really been good—hasn't moved a muscle for me all this time," I said, wrapping my arms around the mare's neck and burying my steaming face in her mane. She whuffled softly as she nosed my bottom, then returned to her hay.

He stroked the mare while he looked over her back at the premature foal sleeping in the straw.

"Is he nursing yet?"

"His suck reflex is improving a little, but we're still tubing him with colostrum every few hours," I said.

"Want to learn a faster way to milk a mare?"

"You bet." He had my full attention, now.

"Sit down and put that leg up while I do this."

I sat, thankful to get my weight off it for a moment, while he searched the cabinet drawers for a big syringe and pulled the plunger out.

"You cut off the business end of the clear part, here," he said, as he sliced neatly through the tough plastic with what had to be the sharpest pocket knife in existence, "then turn the plunger around." When he finished, he handed the contraption to me.

I stared at it, with no idea how to begin.

"You place the smooth end around the mare's teat," Kit said, "and slowly draw down on the plunger."

"Seriously?" I jumped to my feet with a wince and tried it. With only gentle pressure on the plunger, the golden, syrupy colostrum just *flowed* into the syringe. I shook my head and swore softly.

"Works, doesn't it?" He grinned.

"I can't believe it," I breathed. "Thank you so much." If he wasn't my hero before, he surely was now.

"That should speed it up a little."

I filled the rest of my container in three minutes flat. "I've spent… you don't want to know how long…getting that same volume…" My voice dwindled off and I gazed at him. If student ICU techs hugged residents, I would have.

He took one look at me, then backed away, the beginnings of a smile running screaming from his face.

"Good, well—" he muttered, and spun toward the patient bulletin board, his knuckles so white on the pen in his hand, I thought I'd be cleaning up plastic fragments.

I shook my head and filled another container with the precious golden liquid while he stared fixedly at the pink treatment sheets. His fingers had relaxed, and now he merely played with his pager buttons.

"How is that mare, Charlotte, over in C-Barn?" he called across the room.

"I'm on my way over there now, thanks to your milking gadget. Without it, I'd have been ages longer."

His narrowed brows softened and the corners of his mouth even lifted a little.

"No worries," he said.

I stifled a chuckle. Sounded like he'd been hanging out with the new Kiwi Equine Repro resident. New Zealand idioms were popping up all over the vet school. I covered the beakers of colostrum, put one into the fridge, and left the other out for the little guy's next feed.

"So why," he remarked, under his breath, "the heck are you working? You should have that leg up somewhere, not running around barns making it worse."

"I already told you why," I hissed, glancing around. "It's been up long enough. Time for exercise, Doc. Soon I'll be a hundred percent again."

He shook his head.

"You said you were a farrier before you became a vet," I said, changing the subject.

"Yes, I was. Why?" He looked sideways at me, then turned back at the wall before him.

"I spend as much time in the farrier shop here as Sean will have me, but they're all client horses, so I can't trim them. I'd like to learn."

He flicked a glance my way.

"Why do you want to trim feet? You're training to be a vet, not a shoer."

"Horses depend on their feet for their living. It's important they're right."

"It's a lot like hard work." His brow wrinkled and he looked away for a moment.

"Way I figure it," I said, "horse vets need to know about feet. The fastest way to lose an owner's confidence is to mangle a shoe removal or basic trim. I don't want to be a farrier, but I'd sure like to be able to pull a shoe and decently trim and balance a hoof."

He pivoted slowly toward me and his eyes lit up, his lips slowly forming a twisted grin.

I couldn't help beaming back. Encouraged, I rattled on.

"I've spent a lot of time reading about feet, but I haven't had the opportunity to actually trim them." I fell silent for a moment, waiting, but Kit didn't offer.

He turned away and began to sift through a pile of records on the table beside him.

I took a deep breath and let it out, then spun slowly toward a fridge and stared at it, unseeing.

"Guess I'll have to take a farrier course when I'm done with vet school. Doesn't look like I'll learn much about trimming here," I mumbled, half to myself, half to the fridge.

Behind me, Kit sighed.

"I could teach you," he said.

I whipped my head around to stare at him, just as he blinked as if he didn't quite believe what he'd just said.

"Would you? Would you really?" I was stunned. I truly hadn't expected his help.

He swallowed hard, then nodded.

"Yep," he said. "There are plenty of horses in the research herds that could use a bit of attention."

"When can we start?" I was so excited, I nearly forgot to breathe.

His jaw tensed as he held his own breath in silence for long moments.

"I'll make you a deal," he finally said.

I narrowed my brows at him. This couldn't be good. "You do only what you absolutely must on that leg for two more weeks, and then *if* it's significantly better, I'll take you out and teach you to trim feet. Mind you, they're pretty unkempt and they'll be a bit rough to handle—"

"—oh please?" I interrupted. Oh cripes, I was begging to do *feet*…but I meant it.

"Yes," he sighed, "but remember the conditions, eh?"

"Got it loud and clear, Doc," I said, and hobbled on before him, eager to show him the progress Charlotte had made since he'd changed the heel elevation of the shoe on her injured leg.

"HEY, want to go for some pizza?" one of the girls in my class asked the students standing around me.

"Yeah, let's go. I've got room for one more in my car, Miranda," one of the guys said, as he walked past me to steer her in the right direction, without a glance my way.

I took a deep breath and shook my head, riffling through

my pack for our schedule to see what else I needed to do before heading home.

Maybe I was just born different.

But horses liked me…and men, until they got to know me —usually too well, too soon. And then they'd disappear. I couldn't seem to get that one figured out. My female friends usually kicked me from here to Christmas when I did it… again. I only gave the guys what they asked for… and then they despised me for—

—with a shudder, I saw it—in black and white on the page and my heart hits my boots.

Oh hell.

My cousin's wedding is tomorrow.

More people.

I closed my eyes and sank down onto the nearest planter box.

"You okay?" Jess walked up and dropped her pack next to me. "How's the leg?"

I sighed and let my bag slide to the ground, too. "Okay, but I've a wedding tomorrow."

"Why so glum? I love weddings. I'll go."

"Fine, you go in my place," I said, and gritted my teeth.

"What's not to like about a wedding?" She scrunched her face up.

"Too many people, all in one place."

"But you're an extrovert. You should love weddings."

"Far from it. Just looks like that. I'm pure introvert, through and through, but when your parents and grandparents all have retail stores, it doesn't matter what you are—you still need to serve the customers and *act* extroverted, regardless."

"Probably the best thing they ever did for you—it would have helped you get into vet school."

"Yeah, maybe, but it makes my heart hurt."

"You sure look like an extrovert," she said.

"You'd think so, wouldn't you? I tell myself it doesn't matter what people think of me...but it's not true," I whispered. "Nobody, even *you*, gets that I'm terrified—of what they might say, what they might do. At least horses and dogs love you when they love you, even if it's just cupboard love— and they don't bother to lie or make promises they won't keep."

Jess blinked and stared at me.

"The thought of going to a wedding brought out all that?"

"Well, yes. I mean, the ceremonies are all right. I usually even cry. And the dancing's good, if there's someone there who can swing dance...but the rest isn't so hot...drunk people who want to get close," I shuddered, "and think it's okay because it's a wedding."

"True. You don't do drunks, period. I've seen that." Jess put an arm over my shoulders and gave me a hug.

"I can usually escape into a kitchen," I said, with a hint of a grin. "I hate weddings with caterers, though. No escape hatch."

"Didn't you used to work for a catering company when you were an undergraduate? How'd you deal with weddings then?"

"They didn't maul the kitchen minions. Hey," I grinned, "that's an idea. I can take along a black skirt and white blouse...and just disappear into the woodwork."

"So, where is it?" Jess said, shaking her head and chuckling.

"At my Aunt's ranch."

"What's wrong with that? She's the one with all the horses, right? If the kitchen trick doesn't work, you could always head for the stables."

"That's why I love you so much, Jess. You get it."

"Yep," she said. "Are you done feeling sorry for yourself? Because I'm hungry."

"Aren't you always?"

She beamed back at me. She's a tall, gorgeous beanpole and eats whatever she wants. I am eternally jealous.

"OH, LENA, HOW'S SUNSHINE BEEN?" The new resident, Dr. Masters, nodded at a post-op colic horse standing in the ICU stall before her. The palomino had one hind leg cocked and his tail lazily twitched at a fly.

"He's looking good," I said, with a smile, and reached for a second fluid bottle. "He grazes well, ate his feed tonight, and started my shift with a full flake of hay. It's half gone now."

"Good, so he's eating again..." Dr. Masters looked down at the horse's record in her hand and cocked her head, brows coming together a little. "Have you been writing up the records?"

"If I can squeeze in the time, I do." My face heated, and I bit my lip.

Did she mind?

"As busy as it is today? You don't have to do that," she said. "It's my job to write them from your treatment sheets entries. You have enough to do."

I blinked.

"Seriously? You residents never even get time to sleep. If you'd rather write them up, that's fine, but if not, I'm happy to help."

"Thanks Lena," she said, with a sigh. "It's appreciated. Make you a deal. If you think it'll be good for your training, go ahead and do them. I'll critique and sign them off."

"Really?"

"Sure. Happy to."

"I'm after all the practice I can get," I said, as Dr. Masters picked up a stack of records and ferried them toward the office.

I jumped when I saw Kit already there, head down over his papers, scribbling for all he was worth. I hadn't seen him come in. Butterflies bashing to escape my stomach walls, I shivered and turned on my bad leg with two, five-liter glass fluid bottles in my arms. I barely managed to keep my feet, and the profanity under my breath, on my way to the barns. I really must learn to pay attention, even if the illustrious Dr. Allen was present.

Our residents, all of them, make me smile. For people, they're pretty awesome, especially after my exposure to the wedding crowd last week. I survived it, but only just. Ended up grooming horses in my silk dress. By the end of it, I could have come out of the pages of a Thelwell book—the sequence of drawings where a tidy rider begins all dressed for a show with the shaggy, muddy beast she'd evidently just pulled from the paddock... and their magical transformation to a gleaming, braided pony beside an exhausted and filthy ragamuffin with a trashed riding habit.

In C-Barn, I pulled the rope to raise the caged fluid bottle high above Cotillion. The palomino swung her head around and whickered at someone's approach.

Kit. My heart jerked and I swallowed hard.

He reached out to the mare and she lipped at his fingers as our eyes met and held.

"How's she going?"

"Her IV drip had stopped, but I've fixed it," I said. "She's looking a lot brighter than yesterday."

"You know, you don't have to write up records." Kit looked sideways at me.

"I don't have long until I'll be practicing. I need all the help I can get."

"You're doing pretty damn well already," Kit said, his brows lowering. "Most third year students haven't even *tried* procedures you do every shift as an ICU tech."

"Yeah, well, that's why I wanted to work here," I said. "Even with this hospital's big equine case load, the time in clinics is too short for me. I'm a bit slow to learn things."

He rolled his eyes at that.

"You're doing just what you need to be doing, and makin' a good job of it."

"It'd be nice if other people thought so," I said, biting my lip. The black plastic cap from the new fluid bottle clicked into place as I shoved it onto the empty one.

"Who doesn't think so?"

"Nobody," I said, to my feet.

"Who?"

"I'm a pain in the neck, apparently, to my class."

"I'd bet no resident or prof would say that," Kit said, but he squirmed a little.

I swallowed hard. Guess he thought so, too. Must be my questions in class. I truly didn't do it to show off. I just wanted to understand. If I learned it wrong the first time...

"Maybe if you kept your head down a little in cla—" Kit started.

"Seriously, you too?" I shook my head.

And I'd thought...but that wasn't worth thinking about, clearly. "Is there anything else you'd like to know about this horse, Dr. Allen?" I asked, in my iciest tone.

"Now don't go gettin' all huffy, I'm only trying to help."

"Thank you for your concern." I don't imagine it sounded overly grateful, coming from between gritted teeth.

He closed his eyes and inhaled deeply.

"Okay, if you want to be that way about it," he said. "Thanks, anyway, for taking such good care of the horses."

"Any time," I spat out, tucked my bottles beneath my

arms, and bolted for B-Barn, the hemostats and stethoscope clipped to my scrubs swinging with every hop.

MY ALARM SHOCKED me out of whatever pleasant dream had cocooned me. I smacked it on its head, then lay blinking at the sunshine streaming through the jasmine vines that waved in the open window. Their sweet, heady scent was heavy in the early morning air. I rolled over, then sat bolt upright.

Today was the day.

My two weeks of penance were up. I had an appointment to make with a certain resident to trim feet. I stilled, though, thinking about our last meeting. I'd certainly have to apologize. I should've done it last week, but what can I say? I was gutless. After a deep breath to settle my butterflies into place, I shot out of bed and leapt into my clothes.

"What's the hurry, girl? It's early yet," Tamarah said, dodging the gooey tennis ball the Labrador spat at her from two feet away.

"Susie's aim is improving." I laughed. "Soon she won't miss. I'm off."

"You really *are* better," she said, looking down at my leg.

"Amazing what a little water, sitting in the sun massaging, and jumping rope has done." Most of the odd colors were gone and it was down to nearly normal size.

"So, can you ride your bike yet?"

"Did it yesterday," I nodded, pouring uncooked oats into a bowl. "Felt fine."

"One lucky girl," she said, and disappeared into her room, followed by the bouncing dog.

I wolfed my breakfast and shot across town. The only fly in the ointment was my treatment of Kit the other day. I chewed my lip over it while I waited outside K—I shook my head at myself—*Dr. Allen's* office door. He arrived after only a few minutes, so I didn't have long to stew.

"You all right?" He gave me a quizzical look.

"If I were any better, I'd be twins." Cocky cover-up, with the butterflies bashing away inside me and my face doubtless bright red. "Um…Dr. Allen," I groped for words, while I fisted the sides of my shirt, "I'm sorry about my attitude last week." I dropped my eyes to the linoleum. "I had no call to jump down your throat like that—I'm just—a bit sensitive about the topic."

"It's okay, I understand." Kit tried for a smile and shook his head, then he glanced down at my leg, below my running shorts. And froze in his fumbling with his door key. "What have you done with it?"

"Worked on it? It's much better…" My heart sank. I *thought* it looked better…but maybe I was getting ahead of myself.

"It's amazing." He blinked and stared again. "I've never seen bruises change that fast. How'd you do it?"

"I had motivation," I said, resuming breathing again. I told him how, then continued. "I…I wanted to see if we could please make a time to go out and do feet."

"You sure you're ready for that?" He winced, glancing at the offending leg.

"I can jump rope, I rode my bicycle over here, and I've been working."

"There's still swelling on the front of the shin."

"It seems to be a split muscle—it sits over the top now, see?" I propped my foot up on a handy chair and showed him.

"You're right," he said, his face coloring. "Well, I guess we've got a date."

I gulped, at the same time he shuddered and stepped backward.

"Ah…" I said, backpaddling.

"Let me check my calendar," he said in a rush, then tried a few more times to get the key into the lock.

If we weren't both so uncomfortable, it would have been comic. As for me, tempting as he might be, it was time to take care of myself—and that didn't include getting my heart burned again.

For quite some time in the foreseeable future.

4

"You point your toes together, like this, and rest her hoof on your knees," Kit said, using one hand, while he tucked the mare's looped leadrope into his back pocket with the other. The shaggy chestnut, covered in mud, nuzzled his rear and stood like a rock. I'd never seen feet in this condition: long, broken up, and stinky.

Kit's shoeing apron, its leather cut and scarred by years of knives, nails, and fire, was strapped around his waist. Reaching into one of its narrow pockets, he withdrew a knife, the wicked edge curved, with a tiny arc in the end.

"Have you sharpened that thing lately?" I said.

"Every time I take it out," he said, as he slid a sharpener from a pocket on the other side of the apron and wiped it a few times across the front side of the blade, then once across the back.

I blinked.

"Is that all you do to sharpen it?"

"It's diamond," he grinned, "that's all it takes."

I must've looked as dubious as I felt, because he held it out to me.

"Check it out for yourself. Be careful."

I touched the—very sharp—edge.

"I can see another item jumping onto my wish list."

He grinned, then trimmed the hoof, explaining his method, step by step. The muck and flaky old sole flicked out under his flying knife, then he nipped around the wall from toe to heel, toe to heel. A final rasp of the sole, checking the levels carefully against the heel bulbs, then he slipped out from under the horse, crouched under her neck, and trimmed the flares from the dorsal, medial and lateral walls. A few swoops around the edges to prevent chipping, and he offered the hoof back to the mare. She sighed and dropped her head, closing her eyes.

"Bet she can't wait for you to do the next one." I smiled at Kit and my face heated when he returned it.

Those butterflies. All it took was a smile. I shook my head.

"You can finish her feet. I think she's the nicest one of the lot. Some of the others are…probably not ideal for your first trim."

I can do this. Piece of cake.

WELL, it *looked* like a piece of cake. And I'm sure it would be…in my dreams, or after years of practice. It must've taken me a good half-hour to do the next foot. Awfully pleased it was a cool evening, I wiped the sweat dripping from my brow with the back of my forearm—my hands stank of thrush—and set the hoof down gently, as Kit had done. Leaning against the mare for a moment, I peeked over her back at the rodeo going on fifteen feet away and straightened up.

"Do you want me to hold her?" I said, softly.

"Naw, she'll be okay, she's just young. I don't think she's

been broken in," he said, with a chuckle, still trimming, as the filly bounced around.

Sure enough, within minutes, she was standing like a statue, her nose against his jeans. She started chewing on his belt and never moved her legs again, except to pick up her feet. "Someone must have worked with her, though. She doesn't mind my picking up her hind legs." He set her foot down. "And see here?" he pointed with the tip of his hoof knife.

I sidled over slowly and looked at the horizontal slit just below the hair above one hoof.

"She had a reason to object," he said. "She's had an abscess blow out the coronary band recently and the hoof is still painful."

"Do we need to do anything with it?"

"We might have helped her last week, but it's already burst. She'll be okay now."

I shook my head and sighed. He'd trimmed that filly, green as she was, in the time it took me to trim one hoof.

I'd better get back to it.

By the time I picked up the chestnut mare's last hoof, he'd done another two horses. I was slowing down and the sweat poured off me. My legs shook so hard, I could barely control them.

Frankly, I thought I might die before I finished that last hoof, but even that was preferable to having Kit see me quit. Simply not an option.

He wandered over, fresh as a daisy. He'd done another horse while I struggled to finish the mare's final foot.

I stood up, hands on hips, stretching my back out, and took a deep breath.

"I did it. Could you please check her?"

"You sure did." His grin stretched from ear to ear as he looked at my heated face, then he spied my muddy hands, tinged with red. "Uh-oh. You need gloves, next time," he said, as he reached for one of the hooves I'd trimmed. "Good job."

"Thanks, but I'm sure I could do better. What can I do next time to improve the trim, Dr. Allen?"

"Pretty good job for the first time," he smiled, "but since you asked…" He showed me where I could take a little more or a little less on each foot. "Not bad, though. Better than most beginners."

Those words were keepers. True keepers. Worth the sweat…and the blood. Not so sure I wanted the tears, though…I'd have to keep my wits about me…and my heart under lock and key. It seemed to be slipping away again.

"And I think we can drop the Dr. Allen bit, okay?" His green eyes glowed up at me from beside the hoof he was perusing and my heart wrenched.

Could I? *Should* I?

"Okay… *Kit.*" How could I say no?

A little voice started screaming at me in my head and I ignored it. Maybe this could be different…maybe we could be really good friends. A tightening in my abdomen told me how very much I was lying to myself.

I was in serious trouble.

His voice brought me back to reality, or safety, anyway.

"These horses really need some attention. The herd managers try, but there are an awful lot of ponies here.

What about teeth? Want to learn to float teeth? I'm sure they need care too. Here, I'll show you how to check teeth."

With that, he rubbed my chestnut's forehead for a moment, breathing deeply and slowly, then held her halter in his left hand and slipped his right arm into her mouth, up to his elbow.

"Kit." I barely got out the word. Those cheek teeth were deadly.

He glanced around at my tone, then smiled.

"It's all right. I'm pushing her tongue out of the way and in between her opposite teeth with the back of my arm. She won't bite her own tongue, so she shouldn't bite me. Just, for goodness' sake, keep your fingers right back, or you won't have any."

I shook inside, but stuffed it down deep and inspired slowly. In, out…and the mare stood still for me and never moved her head when I did as he instructed.

"Man, the inside edges of her lower teeth are sharp as knives, and so uneven," I said.

"Sure are. Those overgrowths are nasty. Hop out of there and I'll show you how to check the outsides."

Only too happy to oblige, I watched him slide his fingers between her teeth and cheeks.

"You can't safely feel the back ones this way, and you can still get bitten, but just keep those fingers arced back. To really see what's going on in there, you need a full mouth speculum and a light."

"Rinsing out her mouth first would go a long way to letting you actually see what was in there, too," I said, wiping green, grassy slime from the mare's mouth onto my jeans.

"You got it. So, you keen to do more feet and some teeth?"

I took a deep breath.

"Yes, please. Just give me a few days to get over this one. Sorry to be a wimp."

"You're not a wimp and you did a great job. Tomorrow you'll be stiff, and the day after, worse. How about three days from now?"

"Sure. I'm a glutton for punishment," I said, laughing, as I scratched the mare's forehead again. We packed up our gear and headed for the gate.

I couldn't remember being this tired for a long time, but I was happy. It would all be worth it. And I'd get to spend more time with Kit.

"So, how's that roan of yours?" he said, and his lips tightened, as we neared the truck.

"Mickey? He's…good." Silence. "I'm afraid to get back on him," I admitted, finally.

"Look, I know you're keen on him," he looked across at me and shook his head, "but why*ever* do you keep a horse like that?" Kit held his breath as I fumbled for an answer.

"I dunno—I could afford him—and he needed a home. He's a little like me."

He blinked, brows coming together. "Pardon?"

"Not feeling sorry for myself, but nobody really wants me around either."

"What do you mean?" He glanced sharply at me. "You're drop-dead-gorgeous. There must be plenty of guys after you."

"Yep," I finally said, peering at him from the corners of my eyes. "but only for one thing."

"I can't believe that," Kit said, but his tone didn't sound very convincing. At least he seemed to like me for something besides *that*.

"So, what is it about horses that you like so much?" he said.

I blinked at that. What was he getting at? I flicked a glance at his wrinkled brow. It sounded like he really wanted to know.

"I don't know," I hesitated before going on, "I seem to only be happy around horses, and a few people. Most people scare me. I'd rather *stay* away than be pushed away, so I do. Horses, though…I guess I only feel in control of my world when I'm on a horse."

"I have to say," Kit turned to me and our eyes locked, "I get it. Me, too."

It warmed a little spot in my very cold heart to hear his words. I was so lucky to have found him, *as a friend*. I kicked myself. I had to stop this. He was my teacher. I needed to remember. Work hard and learn. Horses had done everything for me. I owed them that.

"WHAT TIME ARE we leaving for Lake Berrymore on Saturday?" my classmate Simon said, to no one in particular in the group of students waiting for class outside the foyer. I bit my lip and chanced a glance toward him. He avoided my gaze and looked at the girl beside me. I hung around the edge of the circle, hoping to be invited... I'd learned my lesson the last time I'd invited myself.

"Sure, you can come along," one of them had said, then gave me the cold shoulder for the whole day. I'd love to have gone this time—town was blinkin' hot this time of year, but it just wasn't worth it.

Maybe I was too soft, but then again, maybe I *was* a pain in the behind.

"You just try too hard," Jess had said, when I'd asked if they really thought that of me. I closed my eyes. I've been trying hard for so long, I guess I don't know how to stop.

I could always go to the barns between classes and see the horses. They were usually happy for an extra pat or scratch behind the ears. Horses, I could do... people, not so much.

My day was about to improve, though, heat or no heat. I had a hoof-trimming date with Kit. I jumped into my truck with more energy than I'd had all day and drove out to the clinics. He was coming out the front door as I drove into one of the visitor's slots.

"Hey Doc, want a ride?"

"Sure." He smiled and motioned toward his own pickup. "Let me dump the pack and get my shoeing gear."

That smile always got me right in the solar plexus, and I struggled for a breath.

Kit slammed the door on his truck and hopped into mine, then sighed and rubbed his eyes.

"Long day?" I gazed over at him.

"Yep, but at least there were horses in it," he said. "Man after my own heart," I said with a grin, then froze as my chest tightened even more.

He flinched too.

Better watch my words.

"WE'VE TRIMMED QUITE A FEW TODAY," Kit said, with a smile, after we'd finished the trims. "We'll work our way through the lot, at this rate."

"It was easier this time." I wiped my brow with a glance at the setting sun. "The horses cooperated beautifully, and wearing a sweatband on each wrist was truly inspired."

"You did well today," he said, as he rolled up the rasps and nippers in his apron and stuffed the extra hoof knives into his back pocket.

"It must be the teacher," I shook my head, "you still trimmed three times as many as I did."

"How many years have I been doing this? Something like eighteen? Give yourself some credit. Your quality and speed are improving by leaps and bounds. And," he reached for my hand and turned it over, gazing at it, "you even remembered your gloves. No blood."

I managed to breathe again after he released my hand. Trying not to grin like an idiot, I unlocked the truck door and pulled a jacket over my clammy torso, still damp with sweat. For a stationary activity, hoof trimming sure took it out of me. I dragged myself into the cab and began to shake like a leaf.

Forcing the fingers of one hand to bend around the

steering wheel, I turned the key and gave thanks when she started.

Kit hopped into the passenger seat and glanced at me. "You cold?" He reached for the dashboard controls.

"Let's get this heater going."

"Don't bother." I gave him a rueful grin. "She takes more time to warm up than we have to get home. I'll be fine when I defrost."

"When did you get so cold?"

"I don't know, on the walk from the back of the facility, I think." The chill of the evening seemed to have penetrated all the way to my core.

"When did you last eat?"

"Mmmm... must've been lunch."

"Well it's after nine now—you've got no blood sugar, woman."

"Guess I forgot."

"How could you forget to eat?" He stared in amazement.

"I was so excited about going out to trim feet, I neglected to grab a snack."

"Well, you're keen, anyway," he said with a grin, as our eyes met and held. "You sure give it your all, don't you?"

"You'd know about that," I said.

"No, you really put your whole heart and soul into everything you do."

"Yeah...whatever it is...heart and soul. Not always the smartest thing, I've discovered."

As it predisposed me to disaster in relationships.

I needed to remember my place, and his, despite what my conniving little heart was saying.

No more crash and burn. It took more energy than I had to lose.

BY THE TIME a new week came around, I thought I might be ready for another go-round of hoof trimming.

The pager at my hip beeped. I smiled, my heart surging, and reached for the answer button. Veterinarians wore pagers. Doubtless, down the road I'd curse them for intruding on my life, but for now, I reveled in packing one.

"Lena, can you please report to Equine Surgery II? Surgeon needs assistance. An ICU tech is on her way to assume your duties in ICU," came the sweet voice of the receptionist.

Odd. That'd never happened before on a shift. I hustled over to the surgery suite beside ICU and slipped quietly in the door, careful not to spook a half-sedated horse. Sunlight streamed through onto the surgeon's—Kit's—surgical field.

He lifted his head and glanced my way.

"Oh, Lena, you've come from ICU? That was quick." He turned back to the rear end of a mare and nodded at a tray with a sterile gown and gloves laid out on a nearby tray. The mare's head lolled as she leaned against the steel stocks, sleepy with sedation. "Ever seen an ovariectomy?"

"We did them in lab last quarter," I said, with a nod. "Can you scrub up, please? Two of my surgery techs have come down sick this afternoon," Kit said, "and I could use some help. Not a lot of room in this girl, but she has a big ovarian tumor and we need to get it out."

"Sure," I said, and headed for the sink.

"Size seven gloves?" Sue, the remaining surgery tech, picked out a packet of sterile gloves, then held up a gown for me to slip into after I'd scrubbed. She tied it while I donned the gloves, biting my tongue as I tugged the ends up over my sleeves.

"We're using a colpotomy approach. Even as big as the ovarian tumor is, I think we can get the ecraseur around it to remove it," he said, as he slipped the instrument inside the mare's vagina and through the incision in its wall. "I've blocked the ovarian pedicle and Sue's already attached sterile umbilical tapes to the clamps. We need to place the clamps onto the mass before we cut it loose."

I smiled my thanks at Sue.

"Your job will be holding on to those tapes," Kit continued, "so it doesn't get away from us inside the abdomen. I don't think I need to tell you what a disaster that might be."

"I'll not let go," I said, with a shudder.

The surgery went smooth as silk, the only difficulty being the sheer size of the massive tumor, the removal of which required enlargement of Kit's vaginal wall incision.

"She ought to start feeling more herself, or *less* of herself, as the case may be, when the hormones from that tumor get out of her bloodstream." He smiled and stretched his arms up over his head. The mare was small, and with Kit's height, he'd been crouched over for the past hour. "She's been acting more and more like a stallion for the past few years as the tumor grew."

"Granulosa-theca cell tumor?"

"Probably. Her testosterone levels from that tumor were sky high," he said, giving her a pat and picking up her record. While he scribbled, I helped Sue tidy the mare and clean instruments.

"It must be time for lunch," Kit said, and glanced at the clock. "Oh hell, it's already four o'clock."

"Thought I was getting hungry," I murmured.

"Let's go get some food. I'll finish this record afterward," he said.

—*beep, beep, beep, beep.*

"Dr. Allen, emergency, please call the front desk, emergency, please call the front desk."

He turned to the phone on the wall beside him. While he listened, he turned and assessed the room. His eyes stared at the other set of standing stocks and he frowned. "Okay, send them over, I'll take care of it. Yes, I have help. Thanks."

"Another surgery?" I said, with a smile.

"Yes, but I'm about to pass out. How about you go over to the cafeteria," he fumbled in his pocket and pulled out a few bills, "and get us both some lunch? I owe you. I'll be keeping you past your quitting time, if you want to stay and help. Do you mind?"

"Not at all. I'll be right back." I grabbed the money and trotted out the door. Stop work when I could assist with a surgery? No way.

I was nearly skipping when I returned with our lunch, halfway through my ham and Swiss on rye. I peeked in the door as before and froze in my tracks.

A perfectly white mare, or she would have been, if she hadn't been drenched with dark sweat, stood shaking in the stocks. Her tail was bandaged, her vulva visibly distended, and her huge abdomen barely fit between the rails. Sue was busy suturing the mare's jugular catheter into place.

My stomach flipped over and I gripped the door. Stars swam before my eyes as sweat broke out on my forehead. I had to leave.

"Lena, good, you're back. Thanks. I need a few bites before I scrub up," Kit said, white-lipped. He flashed a brief smile my way as he accepted the sandwich and tore the wrapping off one end.

"Kit... what..." I began, and fell silent as Kit glared at a greasy, weasel-eyed man that slipped past us and out the door.

"I told him to leave before I made him," he spat out, between bites.

I stared at Kit. I'd never seen his face so red, or the vessels beneath the skin so distended.

"Bastard's been trying to pull this foal since before breakfast. He's a farm manager. Thought he might call his vet sometime this afternoon. Experienced vet, thankfully. Took one feel and sent them straight here. Foal's got a wry neck and it's huge, so we're going straight in her side."

"Why isn't she going in for a ventral midline cesarean?" I whispered.

"He won't let us. Mare's worth forty-five grand, and the foal probably more, but he's told the owner it can come out standing, and that's that. All the anesthetists are tied up in surgery, but it's no big deal. She's already sedated." He gritted his teeth as he filled a syringe with lidocaine and began to block the mare's left paralumbar area.

"I'm not so good with…" I murmured, as I swayed, fear striking cold through my body.

"Got some food?" He glanced at my half-eaten sandwich. "Good. Gown up, this mare's been through enough."

Sue was prepping the surgical site, but I managed to get a gown on alone. The gloves kept sticking on my clammy, shaking hands and they nearly escaped my grasp as I attempted to pull them on in some sort of a sterile manner. I didn't think I'd win, but then they were on. I tried to focus, working by rote, as my mind went blind. I couldn't breathe, then I was breathing too fast.

"What's the matter with you?" he growled. "You're not sick too? Feverish?"

I shook my head.

"Is it the horse?"

A muscle twitched rhythmically beside Kit's eye and I tried to focus on it as I nodded, struggling to clear my vision and get rid of the stars floating before me.

Then he snapped.

"If you can't stand surgery, what the hell are you here for?" he barked.

I gritted my teeth and turned away, then rolled the surgical tray closer and stared at the instruments. I found I could watch as the shaved skin split cleanly from the scalpel. I could hand him the correct instruments: the blunt scissors to make his way through the planes of three muscle layers, sharp instruments for the peritoneum. I could hold the stay sutures exteriorizing the uterus, but when I saw the foal—who would never breathe in its life—I lost it. Full hyperventilation and tears.

"Sue! Get her out of here and get someone else to help," I heard, as hands propelled me from the surgical field and out the door. His look of disgust remained and haunted me.

5

I ran for the ladies' room and slumped to the floor by the toilet, again. Half an hour later, I skulked back, hoping it was all over.

I couldn't forget the look on Kit's face. He glanced around when I opened the door, then turned back to finish writing his records. I was halfway finished with the cleanup before he seemed to notice I was there.

"What are you still doing here? Go on home, you're clearly not well."

"I'm okay," I mumbled, glancing at the mare who stood drooping in the stocks. I tried not to see the dead foal, still waiting for someone from pathology to pick up its pathetic little form. "I'll get her more fluids."

"Then get on home," he said, and walked out the door, the last of his sandwich in hand.

The disappointment in his voice sickened me. He was the last person in the world I wanted ashamed of me. I drove myself on to care for the mare for the next hour: warmed her fluids and found brushes and a warm rug from somewhere in the back of ICU. As I wrapped my arms around her neck and cried for her, and probably for me, I finally stopped shaking.

I dreaded what would happen when I caught up with Kit this evening. We'd arranged to trim feet at six. When I showed up in reception, he just stared at me.

"What are you doing here?" His voice was flatter than a pancake.

"We'd arranged to... do feet and teeth... hadn't we?"

"You were sick. I sent you home."

"I'm better now." And I was, but my breath froze in my chest at the look he gave me.

He inhaled deeply and stared at me. "How..." He stopped.

I looked at him and waited, my hands cold with dread, but he didn't continue.

"Shall I get the shoeing gear and some floats from the barn?" I murmured.

He closed his eyes for a moment, his jaw clenched.

"Are you're sure you're okay?"

I nodded and spun away before he changed his mind.

By the time I'd sweated through my first horse, he'd only done three, an improvement over last time. After I'd finished two horses, it was getting dark.

"You've done well," he said, with a grudging tone.

"Thanks. You're a good teacher."

"What was that about, back in the surgery?"

I froze.

I couldn't tell him.

I couldn't tell anyone. They'd never let me graduate if they knew I couldn't handle a foaling.

"I don't know," I murmured. "Must've been some short-acting bug."

He eyed me sideways, but held his peace. He was cordial, but with a new coldness.

Just as well, I reminded myself. Getting too friendly wouldn't do me any good. He was much too handsome, too smooth, and too accomplished to be true… and he was a blinkin' resident, for cripes' sake. I had enough strikes against me to last a lifetime. No more men.

For a long time.

But we could be friends. I'd just stay out of his way for the next few weeks and ensure his ICU treatment sheets were thorough enough that he needn't seek me out.

My plan might work, but the thought of it left a terrible emptiness inside me.

As I scribbled furiously in Kit—*Dr. Allen's* next surgery lecture, I wondered, not for the first time, why someone with my diabolical handwriting bothered taking notes at all. Maybe I'd learn more if I just tried to listen, but then, with Dr Allen in front of the room, I needed all the distraction I could get.

He was speaking on angular limb deformities and surgical intervention in foals, which I could manage. He was easy to follow and I saved my questions in the margins, marked with a big Q—probably the only thing I *could* read—for the end of the period. I thought they were reasonable questions, but maybe they weren't. He answered them, but his cold stare bored right through me, chilling me to the core.

Maybe I'm just imagining it.

Next period was a lab on leg bandaging and administration of equine medications. My classmate, Miranda, the one Jess said had been chasing Kit earlier, was a city girl who'd never touched a horse before veterinary school. The smart old gelding assigned to her had bent his neck around, teeth bared, and she was in a bad place.

"Miranda," I said, and stepped closer, "look out, that

horse is about to b—"

"—I'm fine," she snapped, and muttered, "know-it-all". The horse pulled his head away and looked out the window, as if he'd never even considered misbehaving.

I walked away, shaking my head. Next time, I wouldn't say a thing. The beast could bite her, for all I cared.

From behind me, Miranda mumbled something else. I made out what might have been "resident". After she'd put the horse away, I cornered her and asked what the problem was.

"You think you know everything about horses, don't you? We're all sick to death of it."

My mouth dropped open as the air left my lungs and I struggled to fill them again.

"No, I don't," I said, my lips quivering as I clamped my jaws, trying not to cry, "but it's the only thing I *do* know about, while you and most of the others know a lot about different animals. I can't see inside a cow—they're just a black and white box to me. A dog or cat... they're enigmas, too. Horses are it for me... I just wanted to help you."

Losing the fight against them, tears seeped from my tightly shut eyes.

"Well, don't bother," she snarked, and stormed away.

I slipped out and found a hidden corner around the back of the barn. My weight too heavy for my shaking legs, I slid down the wall, wrapped my arms around my knees, and finally let the tears flow. If that was what they thought of me, how could I face the class tomorrow? For years, I'd told myself it didn't matter what people thought. Through primary school, I'd been the butt of their jokes, their taunts.

Early on, I discovered escapism via books and hid out in the distant reaches of our school fields, or in the library when the weather was foul. I hid, lost in a book: safe and far from their teasing and abuse.

I'd told myself it didn't matter... but it did.

"You really aren't okay, are you?"

My heart froze at Kit's voice behind me. I slowly turned my head, but couldn't draw my eyes from my boots.

"How long have you been here?" I whispered, between sniffs.

"I walked into the lab about five minutes before you had that discussion with your jerk of a classmate."

Now I wanted to die. He'd seen that? Why was he still here?

"I'm so glad tomorrow's the last day of the term." I wrung my hands so hard, my knuckles cracked. "I don't have to see her anymore for the whole summer, or any of them." And then my guts clenched—Jess would be leaving, too, for a preceptorship in her home town. I gritted my teeth and swallowed back the tears.

He cleared his throat, then finally spoke.

"I thought we could go do some trimming. We didn't get to it last week. Those mares need us, with the condition of their feet." He reached a hand down to me.

For once, nothing came out of my mouth when I tried to speak.

"Come on, horses are waiting, Lena," he said, then added softly, "and so am I. I'll wait as long as I have to." I looked up at that. Our eyes met for a heart-stopping moment, then I put my hand in his and he pulled me to my feet.

"Thank you," I said to his shirt buttons, as he stood before me.

"You're so welcome. I used to feel the same way." He hesitated for a moment. "I can do the other animals, but it's the horses I live for," Kit said, as he turned and walked toward the front of the building. He seemed to have forgotten my hand, still in his firm grip. "I wasn't close to my classmates either... or to many other people, for that matter. Let's go see these horses. It's my birthday today, and it's my gift to the horses for my birthday."

I jerked around to face him. "It's mine too."

"Really?"

I nodded and swiped at my nose with one sleeve.

"Oh, sorry. Here," he said, and flicked out the bright flash of a red bandana.

"It's a 104," I said, with the ghost of a grin. "Haven't seen one of those for years. Shows how far from my roots I've slipped."

"104?"

"Our family friend, Jerry, used to call them '104's', because they had a hundred and four uses."

"They sure do." He laughed, then grimaced. "But you probably don't want to know where that handkerchief's been."

"I'm a vet student, remember?"

"How could I forget? Look... ignore that girl. She's feeling insecure and probably a little jealous that you're so good with horses and work in ICU, and everything."

Yeah, and now someone besides her is spending time with you...

"As I've said before, you can be a bit of a pain in the neck," he broke off and squeezed my hand, "but you're a good hand with a horse."

I closed my eyes. That was a start. The faint glimmer in my heart began to glow. I opened my eyes to find him looking askance at me.

"From you, that means a lot," I said, with the hint of a smile.

"I'm serious." He reached out to brush the hair back from my face. "You'll be a great vet. You care."

"So do you." I bit my lips together for a moment. "Watching you with horses and their owners is the best education anyone could ever get. Unlike most of the other residents, you've been out practicing in the real world for years and years—"

"—you don't have to make me feel so old." He twisted his lips.

"No, really, just watching you with them…it makes me believe I could do it, too."

He was silent for a moment.

"Well, that's made my week, thanks, Lena, and my birthday, too, but those other residents, they've done the hard yards too, at other universi—"

I shook my head and opened my mouth to interrupt—

—*beep, beep, beep, beep, beep.*

He let go of my hand and turned his attention to the black and silver box clipped to his latigo belt.

"Dr. Allen, we have a call for you on line four, emergency. Line four, emergency," came the disembodied voice.

"Let's go find a phone. There's one inside," he said, and strode toward the door to the lab. Lucky he'd waited for me— the lab was locked, with my backpack and jacket inside.

"Dr. Allen here," he said, and stood in silence. He scrabbled for a nonexistent pen in his white university-issue pants and stood frowning. I handed him a pen and paper from my bag and he smiled at me as he listened to the voice on the other end of the line. "Can they bring him into the clinic?" Silence for long moments, then "Okay, I'll be out there in," he glanced at his watch, "fifteen minutes. Thanks."

"What is it?" I asked, shouldering my backpack.

He jumped like he'd forgotten I was there and I grinned.

"Oh, yes, colic," he said, looking away, and reached to turn out the lights. "Where's your two-wheeled nag?"

"I took a bus in this morning. I was running late."

He took a step back from me.

"I'll see you around, then? Sorry, we'll have to do feet another time." He walked away, then stopped and stood frozen for a moment, his head bowed, then turned back to me. "Want a ride? I'm... I'm going out past your place."

What just happened?

I chewed my lip, then inhaled sharply and nodded, swallowing with gritted teeth.

"Yes, thanks. I think the buses have finished."

We drove in silence, the bugs committing suicide on the windshield reminding me of why I needed to keep my distance.

"You sticking around, now school's out?" he said, his eyes on the road ahead, or maybe on the bugs.

"Yes, I can get more ICU hours during the summer while people go on their vacations. Suits me. Might even get a chance to get on that horse of mine again."

He glanced at me with a frown.

"The riding school your horse came from should have dealt with that horse years ago," he growled. "He's been a rearer for ages. How did you end up with him?"

"He's usually good with m... " my voice dwindled, and I chewed the inside of my cheek. I stopped before I could stick my foot even further into my mouth and cringed. Rearers tend to have short life expectancies. "I promise, I'll be careful," I mumbled.

"I can help you with him sometime," he said, but his jaw tightened.

"Thanks," I said, swallowing hard.

"Would you like to come along to see this colic?" he asked, but it sounded like he was just being polite. I'd have liked to go on a call, but not like this, whatever *this* was.

"I have to study for an exam tomorrow—it's during the last period of our last day of the term, if you can believe it, but thank you anyway," I murmured.

He let out the breath he'd been holding, and I closed my

eyes and tried to breathe normally. A roller coaster wasn't what I needed right now, or ever again, really.

"Let's try again for the feet if you have time next week?" He'd recovered some of the color in his voice and my traitorous heart surged.

"That would be great." I didn't look at him as I busied myself jamming my jacket into my pack. We drove on in silence, other than the tapping of his thumb on the steering wheel.

Part way home, I caught Kit staring at me across the cab of the truck.

"What?" I said, as a fist curled in my abdomen.

He took a deep breath and held it, then looked away.

"Nothing," he said, when his sea green eyes finally met mine again.

But I knew it wasn't. Nothing between Kit and I seemed like nothing any more. I wondered what would happen, and what it would take to bring it on.

"Well, there you are," he said, pulling up to the curb before my house.

"Happy Birthday, Kit, thanks for the ride, and… thanks for talking with me. I—I appreciate it."

He waved and faced forward, not looking back as he drove away.

"More than you can ever know," I whispered, to the tail lights of his truck as he accelerated away. "Happy Birthday to me."

"Surprise!" Jess and Tamarah yelled, as I walked in the front door.

"We'd started to think you weren't coming home at all,"

Tamarah said, with a laugh, as they dragged me toward the table where a big cake waited, its candles not yet lit.

"Where were you? Your lab should have finished ages ago," Jess narrowed her brow at my face, "and you've been crying."

"Ummm, I had a bit of an altercation with a classmate, then had a meltdown. Kit found me and we've been talking."

"Oh, it's *Kit*, now, is it?" Jess shook her head. "Really?"

I nodded.

"I think it's been that way for a little while, eh, Lena?" Tamarah said.

"You've liked him for long enough. Guess we'll see how it all turns out, but for now, Happy Birthday, to the best friend out," Jess said, as she turned to light the candles.

I DON'T KNOW who said what to whom, but my classmates were, if anything, a little friendlier on that last day of school than they'd been recently. Hopefully, the change would last into our final year. I did want to be friends with them, but rejection scared me too much to put myself out there.

Kit was all business when we met to trim hooves a few weeks later.

"Hey Lena, what do you say we do some dentistry today, instead?"

"Sounds great. We haven't done any in labs, yet."

It wasn't nearly as exhausting as trimming feet, though I'd have given my eye teeth for Kit's height when the horses lifted their heads higher than I could possibly reach. I learned more about dentistry in those three hours than I even knew existed before that. He taught me about the teeth themselves, how to file the sharp points so they didn't cut into the horse's cheeks or tongues as the they chewed, how to reduce overgrowths without exposing the pulps, and the little things you don't see in the textbooks, like only pulling forward when floating the caudal-most teeth in the mouth, to avoid punching a hole in the back of their throats.

"Why don't we do more dentistry in labs?" I wanted to know.

"Guess the powers that be don't think teeth are important." He shook his head. "I'd bet they would if they had a toothache."

"But it's so important…"

"Guess that's why we're out here today, then," he said, and started on the next one.

Dentistry may not have been as wearing as trimming hooves in the hot valley summer sun, but my back locked up something awful that night.

"Next time, we'll work on using both hands symmetrically," he said, with a grin, a few weeks later when we met to trim hooves.

"Great. Only thing I can do with my left is hold a fork, do surgery, or braid my hair." I chuckled.

"You'll learn. Let's get on to these feet." Kit nodded at the first horse. "Go for it."

WITH SCHOOL OUT, I was only at the clinics for my ICU shifts and Kit's time was taken up with surgeries and working on his research project, so we didn't see each other around much. We'd nod at each other in passing and drop our eyes after our glances met. It seemed we were scared to really look at each other.

Good thing I didn't set my heart on him.

Jess had told me as much when I'd called her last night to commiserate. With her gone, it seemed half of the light had left town. Good thing I still had Tamarah and Susie, and the troublesome Mickey.

I closed my eyes and leaned back against the wall, seated on a bale of hay in front of a big barn fan during a break from work.

Oh, hadn't I set my heart on him? Could have fooled me.

With a sigh, I got up and went back into ICU, arriving just in time to help my supervisor place a new catheter on a dark bay Thoroughbred colt.

—*beep, beep, beep*—

I jumped and pressed its button with one hand, crooning softly to the yearling dancing away from me, while I kept an eye on the needle I'd just stuck through the skin beside his jugular.

"Pagers aren't designed to be used around these babies, are they?" I said softly to Frank, who'd somehow kept the colt from leaping too far when I went off.

"Nope," he said, shaking his head.

"I'll answer it as soon as I get this catheter stitched in..." I muttered.

—*beep, beep*—I caught it quicker this time.

"I think they mean it," Frank said. "Go call reception and I'll finish up here."

"On your own?" I scrunched up my face.

"You've already got the local anesthetic blebs in. Truth be told, he'll probably be better away from you and your shrieking pager," he said, with a grin.

When he frowned, the tanned, mustached Frank was a handsome man, but when he smiled, he set all of our hearts fluttering like we were teenagers. He'd been a great dive buddy out on the coast, when I'd had more time last year. Barrels of fun.

"True, thanks," I said, coming back to reality, as I headed for the phone.

"Lena, could you please report to B-Barn?" said the perpetually calm front office lady. "Treatment crew is short handed and urgently needs help. You're the lucky student today, and I've got someone coming in to relieve you. Please leave as soon as you're able."

"No problem, I'll be there shortly." I thanked her and hung up.

"You need to go?" Frank said, when I returned.

"Yes. Treatment crew needs help, but I'm not sure why they've asked for me."

"I told them we weren't busy today."

"Ah. Are you okay here, or should I stay to help?"

"You go ahead. Me and the boy here," he nodded at the colt who was nuzzling his hand, "are just having a man-to-man talk."

"You enjoy that. Just watch his teeth, he's quick," I said with a smile and trotted out the door.

All of our ICU cases were stabled in the facility proper today, so I hadn't been able to get outside as I usually did when we had horses in several barns. I missed the sunshine, but it sure made for an easier shift when I didn't have to run flat out, lugging ten liters of fluids in heavy glass bottles between barns for eight hours. It had been a hot summer, but I'd been so busy since school had let out, I hadn't even made it up to the lake. I'd only had time to care for Mickey and ride him in the arena a little. I took a deep breath and bit my lip. I'd like to do more with the horse, but... Kit had been scarce, so I hadn't asked him for his help. Frankly, I was scared to take the horse out again—and just as afraid to ask Kit.

Living by fear again, eh chick?

I'd bide my time.

Jarrod, the barn manager, glanced up from his clipboard and sighed with relief.

"Thanks for coming over, we needed the help. That

stomach bug has been wiping out my treatment crew students."

"I've got steel guts," I said, beaming.

"Don't tempt fate." He frowned. "We need all the help we can get."

"Sorry. Where do you need me?"

"D-Barn. There are four students between there and C-Barn, but the place is full and they're struggling to keep treatments going on time. You'll be helping Sam."

"No problem. Need anything carted over?"

"Yep, here," he said, handing over a box of patient-labelled bags. "The drugs for new admissions. Not sure where all these horses are coming from, but we're nearly full," he said, as he dashed off.

"Ah, Lena, have you come to save me?" Sam, with a wild look in his eyes and a spray of white liquid drying down the front of his blue scrubs, looked like he'd been having a day of it.

"I'll do my best. I've brought drugs." A smile cracked Sam's visage as I set down the box of meds and started distributing them to the numbered boxes for each stall. "How far have you gotten?"

He pointed at the chart on the wall and handed me a stack of metal patient record clipboards.

"You can start with these, and I'll keep going with my stack," he said, as he grabbed a 35-ml syringe of penicillin and a smaller one of gentamicin. "Wish me luck—this horse hates injections." Sam was trying to be funny, but he was pale beneath his tan.

I got stuck into my treatments. A few hours later, I was nearly through my patients when I walked past stall 23 and my breath froze in my chest. A bay mare lay on her side in the deep straw. Lying down wasn't a problem, but the fact that she appeared to be going into labor *was*.

I raced to the treatment room and scrabbled through the records until I found hers—in the bottom of my pile.

I shuddered and opened her folder. As I read, my whole body started pinging and blood thrashed in my ears. I leaned against a wall and forced myself to keep reading, but the clipboard shook so badly I could hardly read it.

Justice Stakes, 12 yo Bay TB Mare. Overdue foaling, on foal watch.

Due to foal last week.

6

I awoke in darkness, shaking, the smell of molasses heavy and comforting in the air.

Bay mares, gray mares, screaming, bleeding.

I buried my head under my arms and hid from the dreams, but they wouldn't go away.

I didn't know if I slept or passed out, but someone was calling my name.

Kit.

I froze, and then light showed at the doorway.

"Lena?"

I couldn't even call out, but he must have heard me, because he came to my side.

"What are you doing in—are you all right?"

"I think I'm coming down with—" I stopped, my teeth chattering too hard to talk.

"Don't even go there," he growled. "That won't hold water anymore. What the hell's going on?"

I couldn't answer. I could only stare blindly, then my arms, of their own volition, were reaching for him.

He filled his lungs, like someone about to dive into very deep water, as he hesitated. With a shake of his head, he sat down beside me, pulled me into his arms, and held me close against his chest.

"I know you're not a nutcase, Lena, but what's this about? Where did you go? Sam's been struggling here without you and you're hiding away here, a blubbering mess."

I closed my eyes and nodded.

"It's not like you. You're ultra-responsible and super-caring... and this is the second time you've—" He stopped and stared at me, absolutely still. "It's time to get to the bottom of this. I'll help you. Do you understand?"

"Yes," I whispered, and began to cry again.

"Oh Lena, you've got to stop. Tell me, just tell me. It's... mares... isn't it? Foaling m—"

"Stop, don't say it," I groaned, and sobbed into his shirt. "I'll tell you, but no one else can know. I'll...never graduate... if they know I can't manage... a foaling... mare," my voice dwindled to a halt, and I stopped, unable to go on.

He hugged me tight and waited. The man must be the most patient person that ever lived.

"I was fifteen, and full of myself," I started, gulped, then continued. "Friends of the family lived way up in the hills, on the other side of a river with a ford. No power, no phone, total privacy—my kind of place." I flashed him the ghost of a smile. "I loved house sitting for them—milking the goats, playing with the dogs and horses, having a whole valley to myself."

My stomach began to heave again and struggled to get up, but Kit pulled me in closer. I looked up at him, terrified.

"You can do this," he said, his voice kind, but firm. I forced my stomach back where it belonged and tried harder.

"They had three horses, one of them a m-m-mare, who

wasn't d-due for another month, so they thought we'd b-be okay."

Kit gritted his teeth and held me tighter.

"We were near the coast, out behind Pescadero, and a freak storm came in. The river went up, way up. It was over their walking bridge, too. There wasn't a chance of driving their old truck out through it—I was on my own."

"Oh, Lena." Kit swallowed hard.

"There was no one else there, so I tried to help her myself, but I didn't know where to start. Two feet were out, but nothing more. She was pushing, and pushing... I cleaned my arms and tried to see where the head was, but all I found was a chest, and she nearly broke my arm, pushing..." I collapsed against him with a wail and a new rush of tears.

I shook so hard I couldn't think straight, but I knew this was the end. Kit would never talk to me after this, but it didn't matter, I'd be kicked out of school anyway.

"So... what happened?" he finally whispered, against my hair.

"Dead mare, dead foal, and me wishing I were dead too. They came home a day later and found me in my sleeping bag beside her dead body. I wouldn't leave her, even after she died. I can't even think about a foaling without being sick," I said. "They were sorry they hadn't been home, sorry for leaving me there with a near-foaling mare... but it'll never fix it. I couldn't help her. I failed completely and I—"

"—shhh..." He held me hard against him until I ran out of tears, then started again. "Do you know what she died of?" he murmured.

"When the vet could get through, he looked...and said she died of a massive internal bleed."

"Listen to yourself," he said, holding me so tight I could scarcely breathe, his voice shaking.

"What?"

"Listen to yourself. Give me the facts."

"What facts?"

"You were, how old?"

"Fifteen…"

"And how much veterinary training had you had?"

"I still should've been able to help…" I mumbled, but it was starting to sink in.

"And you had how much contact with the outside world? And help?"

I was silent for long minutes.

"None," I finally answered.

"And now you know a bit more about medicine, what could you have done for an internal bleed on a foaling mare in the middle of nowhere, by yourself, even as a full-fledged veterinarian?"

I stopped and stared at him as my head spun, blinking back more tears.

"Not much, I guess, but even knowing that, I still feel like emptying my guts."

"We'll get you through it, if you'll let me help."

I snuggled in closer and breathed deeply of his scent, and my heart lifted, just a little bit.

"But this…" he looked down at me, and at his arms enfolding me, and bit his lip. "I don't know what to say, or even if this is a good idea… at all." He fell silent. "I'm damaged goods too. I don't know if I have any business dragging you into my life, as messed up as I am, either."

"In what way could you ever be messed up?" I turned a wrinkled brow up to him.

"I can't believe I hide it that well," he said, his eyes glistening. He stiffened, then slowly began to talk. "I haven't had anyone to talk with about it, other than my sister, and she's away in some godforsaken country where there aren't phones, piped water, or paved roads."

I had to smile at that. He was even funny when he was miserable.

"I was divorced... just before I bolted back to my alma mater, here. I'm starting over. I lost nearly all the horses, the house, the clinic... my life. Thank god we never had children, or I'd never have borne it." He sat, silent, a tear running down his cheek. "And it was all my fault. She ran around on me, but I did it first."

I stared at him, then slapped my jaw shut.

"I can't believe you'd do that. Not you," I argued.

"I may not have abandoned her for another woman, but I abandoned her nonetheless... for my practice, my clients, my patients. I was there for them... always... but never for her." He swallowed hard, his jaw locked tight. I took a deep breath and held it, then let it out slowly. "So, with nothing left, I came back... back to the place I loved the most, where horses were king and caring for them could be my life... without hurting anyone else... or letting anyone in that could hurt me. It was easier just not to feel..." He stopped and looked down at me. "And then you come along."

"Me?"

"You. You with those sea green eyes..."

"Same as yours," I whispered.

"Same as mine," he agreed. "I tried to leave you alone, stay away... but..." He closed his eyes for a moment.

"Me too."

"And so, you see, I find I want someone to care again... and I want to care about someone... you, specifically. I fought it, damned if I didn't try to keep you away, keep you at arm's length, but you kept coming back for more... your desire to help horses... it was like a drug to me."

I swallowed hard. I wanted it so much, but...

But what?

My memory of why I shouldn't get involved with *anyone* was fading fast.

"I'd always wanted to do a surgery residency here..." Kit hesitated, "and now I'm here and almost done, it's not nearly enough. I want to stay, permanently, to teach... get on a tenure track, become a professor."

"You'll be the best they've ever had."

He let out his breath in a snort. "Hardly," he gave me a soft smile, "but I'd like to think I could at least make a difference to a lot of horses and students."

"You already do that," I said, and leaned harder against his solid chest. "And you're easy to talk to."

"And you understand how I feel about horses."

I tried to look away, but his eyes drew me back.

"But we can't..." It came out on a sob, wrenched from me, unwillingly. "I'm a student, you're faculty."

"There are no written rules on that, by the way," he said, with a twist of his lips. "I checked."

"But it couldn't help your chances with the faculty—it would be 'frowned upon'...and the way I see it, you'll need every point in your favor—plenty of people want tenure here."

"And, as others would say, and maybe they're right, I'm too old and you're too young," he said, with a wistful smile.

"That's not true, actually," I said. "You're over ten years younger than my last fiancé."

He blinked.

"Seriously?"

I nodded.

"And..." I whispered, "the third argument, I don't want to get hurt anymore."

"That makes two of us."

"You'll never get that professorship, though, if you hang around with students, much less sleep with them," I said flatly, and turned my head away. "I don't want to wreck your chances."

"I'm beginning to think it doesn't matter… as much as this…" Kit turned my chin toward him with the side of his finger, then lowered his lips to mine.

I could have fallen into his warm lips, his touch… and I let it happen. I returned his kiss with all the feeling I'd kept hidden for so long.

"So…" I said, panting a bit, when he finally let me breathe again.

"What are we going to do about it, you mean?"

"Yes," I said. My firm tone came out as more of a breathy whisper.

"Well, first, we're going to get you over this fear of foaling."

I gulped and the chill started up in my guts again.

"Hold on, there. It'll be okay. Just hold on. Again, you were how old? And had how much veterinary training?"

"Fifteen, no training."

"Think about this, with your head and not your emotions. Is that reasonable?"

"Y—no," I said, and the tears began to fall again. "But my heart, it just…locks up and I can't breathe, or think."

"We'll fix all that. Deal? I help you do that and you help me fix my heart and learn to trust again?" He was silent for a moment. "Maybe you can start learning to trust again too, eh?"

"That's a big ask, with my history, but—"

"—deal?" he cut in.

"Deal."

I turned my face up to his and we kissed again. He leaned back against the wall, holding me tightly in his arms.

The warmth, the closeness, the safety.

I wanted it to go on forever.

But nothing lasts—I stopped myself.

Why not? Why not you?

That blasted little voice again.

I focused on Kit's eyes. For the first time ever, no vagueness—or had it been avoidance?—showed in their depths. His green eyes were nearly black, intense, close before me.

I froze as a flash of green—a figure in surgical scrubs —showed, silhouetted, in the doorway behind Kit's head. With the click of a door latch, it was gone and I let my breath out.

"Shall we go?" he murmured.

I turned my head back to him and he smiled.

"Go?"

"The next shift will have taken over. It's way past dinner time and I'm sure you haven't eaten. I know this great little place just down the road."

I smiled, as my heart filled to bursting. It had been far too long since I'd heard those words.

"WHAT'S UP WITH *YOU*?" Tamarah nearly dropped her fork as I bounced into the house.

"Had a good day," I said, feeling like my face might crack from the smile plastered across it. "You?"

"I saved you some dinner," she said. "It's on the stove."

"Thanks, I've eaten."

She turned and stared, her brow narrowing as the moments passed.

"What's his name?"

"Kit."

"That's Dr. Allen to you, kiddo, and don't you forget it. Thought you didn't want to be a fly on the windscreen again."

"It won't happen. We understand each other," I said, and swallowed hard, thinking back on the afternoon. "Thanks for saving dinner, I'll take it for lunch tomorrow."

She shook her head and returned to her book while I bit my lip and headed down the hall to my room. It was sad she couldn't be happy for me. Maybe I'd just head over to Mrs. Blakeley's.

With more chocolate chip cookies in my stomach than I wanted to count, I drifted blissfully to sleep, my last thought of Kit's arms around me, his lips on mine.

"Lena!" Tamarah called, her voice sharp, through my open doorway. It was full dark and her bedroom light shone through the curls in her sleep-tousled hair. "Are you okay? You were screaming."

I sat bolt upright, blood pounding in my ears.

"It was... I was... I was running..." I took a deep breath to clear my head and try to still my racing heart. "I must've been dreaming," I said, my voice fading to nothing.

"If you're all right, then," she said, her voice heavy with doubt. "You've never done this before, at least, not that I've heard."

"Thanks, I'm okay. You can go back to bed now."

I didn't want to remember the dream, but it wasn't going anywhere.

Kit was ahead of me, not looking back. I ran as fast as I could, calling out to him, but I'd never catch up, and then a blonde girl was running to meet him. She leapt into his arms and he swung her around and kissed her, for what felt like forever. He never even heard me, as I sank to the grass, my heart bleeding all over the ground before me, screaming, screaming, screaming.

What was all that about?

Whatever it was, I sure wasn't going back to sleep now. With a sigh, I got up to make myself a hot chocolate.

I sat on the living room sofa, huddled around my favorite hand-thrown mug. Surely, I could learn to trust a man again? Would I never be ready? Would it end up like last time? It couldn't. He was nothing like Gareth. I sipped at the chocolate, a warm, comforting smoothness… so much like Kit…

I swore softly beneath my breath. *I had to get a grip.*

Was it crazy to get involved? For me, and for him as well? Mom always listened to her dreams… but did I really have to, this time?

THE WORLD HADN'T ENDED by morning. The sun still rose and the earth still turned, though there were dark bags under my eyes when I glanced in the mirror on my way to work.

When I got there, I was pleased to see a bright little foal beside the bay mare in stall 23. I found Sam and apologized profusely, claiming illness. He looked shattered and I felt guilty as hell.

My nightmare of the previous night had receded to a distant memory, but it kept popping up when I least expected it… like while calculating a fluid dose rate or shaving over a jugular to place a catheter. I shook my head. I tried to convince myself it was just the mare in stall 23.

Living by fear was no way to live.

I SIGHED as I leaned back against the pillows in my room, fondling Blackie. The little cat had adopted me during my second year of college and stayed by my side ever since, moving from one student apartment to the next. When I'd start packing once again, she'd crouch beside her food bowl, hissing and growling from the time she saw the cat box until she was unloaded beside her already-laid out food and water in our new premises. She'd snarl, sniff at her feeders but touch neither, hop onto my bed, glare some more, then finally seek the window I'd always leave open for her.

My chest would tighten when she hopped out and for the next ten to sixteen hours, until she'd jump back in, leap up to her blanket on the end of my bed, groom herself, curl up and go to sleep, one languid eye on me. Nothing else was ever said about it. She was home.

I wish I could make myself comfortable so easily in a new domain, or come to think of it, in an old one. Blackie was a bit of a loner and I guess I was, too. My horses had been my closest friends, growing up in the redwoods. I was never bored, and with the horses, never lonely… or not much, anyway. The horses made up for a lot and I wanted to do my best for them… they'd saved me before. I had to become the best vet I could be.

A tattered edge of parchment peeking from a stack of papers caught my eye and my heart clenched. I rolled off the bed to pull it out. I'd entitled it *"Hold on Tight to Your Dreams"*, with a brown calligraphy pen and artfully burned the little poster's edges. Around the title were short blurbs: *Veterinary School, Hold On, Horse Vet in the Making, Keep on Track, You Can Do It, The Only Goal, It WILL happen if you do what it takes, Vet Med Lasts Forever—Parties Don't*, each followed by exclamation marks.

It had been posted on the wall behind every one of my desks for as long as Blackie'd been in my life. Its statements comprised my mantra. I held it in both hands for long moments, then deliberately pinned it to the wall where it belonged.

I couldn't let it go now, but wasn't I worthy of love, too?

But what would happen to Kit? And his goals? I tipped my head back and closed my eyes.

Three knocks on the door. It opened, and Tamarah stuck her head in.

"Phone for you, sleepyhead. Sounds familiar," she whispered, her hand over the mouthpiece, then bit her lips together and looked at me with her big brown doe eyes. Maybe she was feeling bad about raining on my parade.

"Thanks," I said, and reached for the phone she extended toward me.

The door closed with a click and I put the phone to my ear.

"Hello?" I nearly dropped it when Kit's voice came from the receiver.

"Hi Lena, it's Kit."

"Well, hello," I said, scarcely daring to breathe.

"I wanted to call and say hi. I didn't see you around today, but someone said you looked a little glum. I wondered if you'd like to go out and get a bite to eat. We can go out to Sutherfield Station. They make the best burgers in the county."

I held my breath and blinked until his words got through.

"Out?" I said, still trying to grasp it.

"Yes, like out, like people do, you know? Boy asks girl out to eat, pays for her dinner, that sort of thing. I know you haven't taken much time to do things like that, but you should try it sometime. You might like it."

"Of course, I'd love to," I said, with a chuckle. "Thanks, Kit. I'll be ready."

I swore softly under my breath. Whatever would I wear? I shook my head. The man had only seen me in jeans, shorts and scrubs. It really didn't matter… but it did.

By the time my bed was heaped with discarded clothes, I'd

found the blouse and sweater I wanted to wear over my new Wranglers. With my white cowboy boots I danced in, I might just be presentable.

"Where are you going, dressed like that?" Tamarah's eyes goggled.

"Out for a burger."

"Ummm…" She blinked. "No, not really."

"Yes." I allowed myself a little grin. "Kit."

"Isn't he a bit old for you?" Tamarah glanced at me sideways.

"I like older men."

"And look how an older man turned out last time."

"Blake was a *lot* older." I bit my lip. She'd tried to warn me off then, too.

"Precisely my point. So is Kit." She was a Pitbull, sometimes.

I sighed and met her eyes. "It was his jealousy that got to me, not his age." I shook my head. "Nothing more."

"With age comes a different way of looking at life. And your intolerance"—her brows narrowed at me—"didn't let you see it was just him caring about you."

"That was not why," I said with a glare at my boots. "It meant he didn't trust me."

"Whatever," Tamara growled. "Can't argue with someone who's always right."

"Sorry Jess"—I winced—"let's forget it, eh? Thanks for trying to help."

She was only too glad to oblige. "You just take care," Tamarah said, shaking her head. "I hope you know what you're doing."

"I'm workin' on it," I said, as the doorbell rang and I went to open it. "Bye, Tam. Have a good evening."

I stepped out into the night and my eyes locked with Kit's.

My reservations, whatever those were, melted as Kit took

my hand and squeezed it.

"You look lovely," he said, his eyes warm.

"You don't scrub up so bad yourself, Doc," I replied. "I've never seen you out of uniform, *sir*."

He laughed as he handed me into the passenger seat of his truck. I buckled myself in, but when I glanced up, he still hadn't closed my door. He stood there, just looking at me.

I bit my lip and waited.

Slowly, deliberately, Kit leaned down and kissed my lips. Softly, lovingly.

"I've been wanting to do that all day," he said, adding dryly, "that is, when I wasn't considering running for the next state."

"You too?" I grinned, then sobered.

"I'm glad you still wanted to go out with me tonight," he said, his voice barely audible. "I nearly bolted yesterday when I woke up in the morning. Frankly, I'm terrified... but somehow, I found myself picking up the phone tonight. I swore I wouldn't do it again, but as you see, here I am."

I took his hands and kissed his knuckles. When I could finally think again, I looked up at him.

"I had nightmares last night." I couldn't even admit the contents to myself. I didn't think I could tell him, not yet.

"Sounds like we're about even, then. How about we take it slow?" He swallowed hard and waited for me to speak.

"I-I-I, yes. Slow is good," I said, my voice quavering.

"I'd hoped you'd say that," he murmured, and kissed me again. "All in?" he said and shut the door. "To Sutherfield?" he said, as he slid into his own seat.

I smiled and nodded, taking the hand he reached across the cab to me.

"To Sutherfield."

WHEN I GOT HOME from work the next day, a message was waiting on my bed. My heart plummeted as I read Tamarah's perfect handwriting.

Lena, Dean Jensen from the vet school wants to see you. Please call him back at 719-...

With the events of the past few days, I somehow didn't think it was going to be as nice as our last meeting, a reception for new entrants to the veterinary school's hallowed halls.

7

I called the dean's office first thing and was given an appointment for 0730 the next morning. The secretary had apparently expected me to call.

I'm not sure how I survived that day or slept that night, but nonetheless, I was up before dawn, my head swirling. At risk was everything I'd worked so hard for, this Main Street town-humanities-girl learning sciences and somehow achieving the necessary 3.86 average, working Friday and Saturday night graveyard shifts in emergency clinics while attending university full time. No wonder I was lost when it came to human relationships. I don't know how my married-with-children classmates did it, but they did.

Either way, I might not have to worry about it much longer. My heart slithered into a mess in the bottom of my running shoes as I turned away from a perfectly good breakfast, unable to stomach it. It wasn't light yet, but I needed a run. By the time Danny, Mrs. Blakeley's borrowed Golden Retriever, had loped happily beside me for a good five miles, I'd settled enough to think straight. Not clearly, but straight.

"Are you okay?" Mrs. Blakely asked, frowning, as I handed his lead back to her.

"I'll be better, or not, in a few hours." I tried for a smile, but don't think I made it.

"You be sure to let me know. I'll be baking your chocci-chip cookies today."

"You bet I will. Thanks. I'll see you later." That helped.

Chocolate always does, even just its promise.

I don't remember riding across town to the big man's office. The raised-relief animals on the front of the vet school seemed to be hiding their faces from me this morning. Bad sign.

I was early and Dean Jensen wasn't, so I cooled my heels for fifteen minutes in the waiting room, trying not to finish off my long-suffering fingernails. Finally, the dean's starched secretary showed me in.

"Good morning, sir," I squeaked.

He nodded at a chair beside his desk, while he finished reading the paper in front of him, then turned to me.

"I hear you're not doing your part in the barns."

I blinked.

"Pardon? In ICU?"

He raised a brow at me.

"I understand you're exemplary in class and in ICU; it was your conduct while assisting treatment crew the other day which concerns me."

I sat in silence, staring at him, and my heart hit my boots. *The mare.* I took a deep breath. That was bad enough, but I prayed it wasn't more.

"I understand you skipped out when the other student on roster was already stretched to his limit. That was an expensive mare you were to watch. Her owners put their confidence in us to give her the best of care… and I see," his fingers walked through the stack before him on his desk and plucked out one pink piece of paper, "that you asked the student working with you to help you with the mare… and *disappeared*. Some excuse of not feeling well, but you were seen in *flagrante delicto* some time later, coming out of a storage room—with a man. I don't know what you can possibly say that would make sense of this, but… I'm giving you the benefit of the doubt here. If you're scared of horses, I suggest you petition to change your track to Companion Animal."

I must have stared at him with the horror I felt because his frown nearly cracked to a grin.

"It's not actually a death sentence, being a small animal vet, you know," he said, more softly.

"Of-of course not, sir," I said, racking my brains to remember what his specialty had been prior to his appointment as dean. I gave up and tried to focus as he continued.

"…if you simply cannot be bothered attending to the duties falling upon you as a veterinarian… it just doesn't bear thinking about. I don't know what your problem is, but sort it. You do not have another chance. You've worked hard to get to this point, but this cannot be ignored. It was reported by one of last year's graduates. That is all."

"Thank you, sir," I said, and blindly leapt from the seat and spun to bolt.

From over my shoulder came his voice, hesitant this time.

"And about Dr. All—"

I froze in my tracks, every muscle tensed, as terror washed over my body like a bubbling ice bath.

"Never mind," he said, his voice gruff.

"Thank you, sir," I repeated, sounding like a broken record. I softly closed the door to his chamber and practically ran down the hall toward the safety of *The Granary*. Hope upon hope, Jess would be there. Passing the faculty photos, I had the presence of mind to scan them to discover the species with which Dean Jensen had distinguished himself. A good thing to know in case I had to see him again. Anytime would be too soon. Much too soon.

Whatever were Kit and I to do?

I TRIED to find Kit all that day, but he was in surgery every time I checked, and then I worked until ten. I didn't have his phone number, but I shrank from having him paged—what the heck would I tell the receptionists at the front desk? As the day wore on, my trepidation grew, so... coward that I am, I waited until he called.

Thankfully, a message, complete with his phone number, waited on my bed.

Kit called, please return his call, he'll be up late. 719...

"Thanks, Tam," I whispered as I passed her closed door. She'd be long asleep, after her customary early bedtime.

I managed to control my shaking hands long enough to get him on the phone.

"Hello, Kit here."

"Hi, it's Lena."

"Well hello there, you're back late."

"I was working."

"I know, I saw you, but you were talking with the owners of that pinto. Didn't want to put you off, so I thought we could talk tonight."

"Thanks, and... but... I needed to talk with you," I said in a rush.

He hesitated.

"Is everything... okay?" he murmured.

"Well, other than being called into the dean's office to

discuss my negligent behavior and being told that despite my exemplary record in school and in ICU, I had no more chances left, everything's peachy."

"Oh, Lena. Do you want me to come over?"

"But the worst of it…" I couldn't say it.

"There's worse?"

Silence

"Yes. He started to say something about Dr. All—and then he stopped."

The silence rang through the line and my heart positively stopped. He finally answered.

"No one knows we were together. We've only been out in public to eat."

"No. But… oh." I closed my eyes and sank to my bed. I'd forgotten about whoever it was that'd shown up in the doorway just before Kit and I left the feed room. Miserable, I told him. "And… Dean Jensen said someone reported 'my behavior'."

"It's okay. It was bound to happen. I already told you that you were more important than… all that other stuff." His gulp was audible and his voice wavered a little, but he went on. "We just 'play it cool at school', as they say, and our free time remains our own. We'll get though this, I promise."

"Kit, you're…" I shook my head, "amazing. Whatever did I do to deserve you?" I whispered.

"Just bein' you, lady, just bein' you. So, are you okay now, or do you need me to come over?"

"I'll be fine, I think. I was more afraid of what you'd say."

"What I'd say?"

"Your plans, staying on, professorship."

"We'll deal with that when the time comes. No more about that, deal?"

I bit back a sob and hesitated for a moment.

"Yes," I finally said.

"Hey, I don't have to be in until noon tomorrow, you free in the morning?"

"Yes, till three."

"How about we go for a ride? I can borrow Aspen from Haley in ICU and we can get out."

"I'd love that," I said, my heart filling again. Getting to ride Mickey again and spending time with Kit. What more could a girl want?

"I'll pick you up at seven, eh?"

"I'll be ready," I said, "with bells on."

KIT WAS MORE than a good hand with a horse. Our first time working with Mickey together made a big difference. After that, my fear of riding the beast diminished, though I was still careful.

"I was just thinking," I said, as we walked the horses cool, side by side.

"Good thoughts?"

"You know how you said I put my whole heart and soul into things?"

Kit nodded.

"Well, it happens in relationships, too. It usually scares the crap out of the guy and I never see him again."

"I don't scare that easily," he said, playing with the end of his reins.

"Is that so?"

"Yep."

"I'd started to think it might never happen... ever." I chuckled.

He looked at me and took a deep breath, emotions warring on his face. Finally, he shrugged and shook his head, seeming to come to a decision. His face lightened, and he reached for me.

I slid into his warm embrace, the reins in our hands tangling, and felt at home, truly at home.

His chin rested on my head and his words reverberated through me.

"I swore I wasn't going to get involved with anybody, not for years and years, but you did it. I don't know how, but you did."

"I didn't know I was doing anything," I whispered. "I was just trying to get better for the horses, but I hadn't counted on one tall, dark and handsome resident."

"Guess we're just kinda made for each other."

"We even have the same birthday, fancy that."

"Yeah. Pretty cool, isn't it?"

Mickey stuck his nose in between us and snorted.

"Obnoxious creature, but I kinda like him," Kit said, letting go of me with one hand to rub Mickey under his forelock.

"Trade him for Aspen," I said, as his borrowed sweet little bay Quarter Horse gently placed her nose into my free hand.

"Wish I could," he said. "I would if she were mine, at least until I sort out this great lunk's rearing problem."

I loved having this open friendship, plus a little more at home, while having a secret one at work.

Kit would come in and see me if he had a few minutes. We'd talk about cases, horses, and whatever else came up. If no one was around, he's drop a kiss on my lips or the back of my neck as he walked past. If others were around, a warm glance or a little wave would come my way and I'd have to bury my face in records or some drawer until the flush in my face dissipated. Otherwise, people would certainly be asking questions, with repercussions for him.

As THE END of summer approached, it only got hotter, if that were possible.

"Hey kiddo," Kit said, when I picked up the phone one glorious morning.

"Hey, yourself," I said. "What's up?"

"How about we head for Berrymore? I'm not on call and I didn't see your name on the ICU roster."

"You're on." I grinned. "I'll do lunch."

I packed my bag and our lunch in no time flat and was sitting on my front steps when he drove up.

"You ready?"

"Ready as I'll ever be." I leaned into his open window and kissed his lips.

"Let's go, then! I've left the dogs home. They were not impressed," he said, as I jumped in.

"I'll bet not. Next time?"

He nodded, then inhaled and smiled.

"You smell good enough to eat," he said, reaching over to pull me closer.

"Jasmine."

"My new favorite," he said, with a glance over his shoulder, as he pulled away from the curb.

We drove to the far side of the magnificent lake where we found privacy, a shady tree, and just enough breeze to keep us cool. We munched and spent quite a bit of time in each other's arms, talking and eyeing each other up in our bathing suits.

Kit laughed.

"What?"

"We're so tanned... your legs and arms, my arms, and both of our necks and faces. You'd think we worked all the time."

"We do." I winked at him.

"Not always," he said.

"You always do."

"Do not."

"What's that thing on your jeans?" I said.

He looked at the folded blue denim with his pager on top and narrowed his brows at me.

"You're not on call," I said.

"I'm always on call, well, not officially."

"In your head, you are."

"And that's a problem… why?" he said.

I sat still, considering.

"It's not a problem until it goes off," I said.

"Run that by me again?" He frowned.

"Even when you're not on call and that thing goes off," I searched for the right words, "you…get this heavenly glow to your visage, like you've seen a vision that you want to follow… and then you disappear. Go vacant. It's like nothing else in the world matters." My voice dwindled toward the end. "And it seems, you don't really come back after that."

"I don't…" He froze and his brows drew together as he sat in silence for long moments.

"But…it's so impor—" his eyes shot up to mine. "I-I guess you're right." He paled and sat very still.

I offered my hand and he gripped it tightly.

"I don't want to do it again, lose someone to my," he cleared his throat, "work. Guess I need to remember others *are* on call who can take care of it." He seemed to have to drag the last bit out of himself, with a shudder, and he pulled me onto his lap and held me for long minutes.

"Hangover of your old life? Sole practice?" I whispered into his shirt front.

His chin bumped my head rhythmically as he nodded.

"Yep. And then it became a refuge from an unhappy, abandoned wife."

"Easy to do," I said. "Happens all the time. Plenty of that sort of divorce among professionals."

"So how do we make it work?"

"Maybe staying present, even when that little box screeches?"

He tugged me in closer and kissed me again. It felt wonderful and my heart loved this, but the old unease, the "what-if", was sneaking back in. This felt too good, too easy. Everything in my experience screamed that anything this easy was suspect.

"What's the matter?"

"Just old shadows," I murmured.

"Let's blow 'em out, then. We both have too many of those today. Swim?"

I nodded. He kissed me again and somehow got his legs beneath him, stood, and raced toward the water with me in his arms.

"I don't usually do cold water, but I'll make an exception for you." He laughed, and ran straight in, gasping as he hit the cooler depths, and let me go.

Me, I'm a fish. I don't particularly care about water temperature, but I draw the line at more than a quick dunk if there's ice floating on top. Good Viking, Russian, and Scottish blood, I guess. I have plenty of all three.

I stretched out and floated like a jellyfish while he splashed around. A duck dive, and I swam underwater until he was above me, then I kicked upwards and grabbed him.

"Arggghh!" he yelled, and I popped to the surface with a laugh.

"Sorry, couldn't resist it," I said, with an impish grin.

"How'd you do that? I couldn't find you, thought I'd drowned you."

"I grew up in our creek in the redwoods."

"You didn't learn to swim like that in a creek." He grabbed

me around the waist and we tried, rather unsuccessfully, to tread water together.

"No, I swam with the local master's swim team. I was fit, then."

"You're pretty fit now, did you quit?"

"With a horse and job, on top of vet school, there isn't the brain space, time or money."

"Do you miss it?"

"Sometimes, like now," I said, "but we're here."

"Let's do it again, soon," he said, as our lips met once more.

"HEY," Kit said, a few weeks later, "I have to go up north next month to do some talks about my research, drum up support, and see some people in my old practice area. Want to come?"

"Sure do." I smiled up at him.

"We'd be away for a whole weekend, think you can swing it?"

"With enough notice, I can trade my weekend shifts."

"I'd like to show you some special places… and I'll," he gulped, "leave the pager at the clinic."

I blinked.

"They'll think you've died somewhere," I said. "Isn't it sutured to your side?"

He took a deep breath.

"Feels like cutting off my arm, but I'll give it a go."

I laughed and wrote down the dates he gave me.

"Let's go grab some dinner," Kit said.

"How about I cook you dinner at your place?"

"I'll never say no to a home-cooked meal," he grinned, "but we'll have to go shopping first. There's nothing in my fridge."

I couldn't help feeling like we were an old married couple as we took turns pushing our cart down the aisle of the grocery store. An attendant stocking shelves was blocking traffic, so we pulled aside to let a shopper coming the other way pass first while we discussed the relative merits of vegetable oils. I looked up to see the thunderous visage of Dean Jensen as he passed the stocker. A pink purse in the child seat of his loaded cart adding to the incongruity of seeing the vet school dean in such a mundane place.

I gulped and flicked a glance at Kit, then did my best to sink into the linoleum tiles.

"Miss Scott, Kit," he nodded. He was nearly past when a woman came up behind us and stopped in front of Dr. Jensen's cart.

"Oh, hello Kit! I haven't seen you in ages." The immaculately made up and coiffured woman gripped Kit's sleeve with her perfectly manicured hands, complete with lacquered nails.

Kit recovered first while I hovered behind him.

"Why hello, Mrs. Jensen. It's been quite some time," Kit agreed, and began to sidle away from her.

"And is this your wife?" She made to peer around Kit to see me, and he stepped aside.

"This is Lena Scott," Kit said.

I offered my hand and she shook it. Mine looked rough and unkempt in hers—I had to keep myself from shoving it into my back pocket when she finally let go.

"So lovely to meet you, Lena. It's so interesting how women keep their own names these days, isn't it?" she said, and smiled at her husband, whose scowl hadn't even begun to diminish.

"If you'll excuse us, people, we really must go," Dr. Jensen growled. "It seems we have guests arriving shortly, so we'll be off."

"Lovely to meet you, Mrs. Jensen," I murmured.

"We'll see you soon!" she called over her shoulder, then turned back to her husband. I just caught her comment as the good doctor rushed her away. "Such a lovely couple. We'll have to have them over soon."

Oils forgotten, we scurried the rest of the way along until we turned a corner, then I grabbed Kit's jacket on each side of his waist.

"Tell me we didn't just meet the dean and his wife."

"You're right, he didn't look very pleased."

I took a deep breath to steady myself as my face slowly cooled.

"You sure this is a good idea?" I set my jaw and gulped. I wanted this, but at what cost? Could I be responsible for his lack of advancement, and would he hold it against me later?

That little voice was screeching again.

Let him go.

8

"I said it before, and I meant it." Kit set the bag of groceries onto the counter in his minute kitchen. "You're more important than a university position. Heck with them if they think it means I'll be a bad professor. It's not like the faculty don't engage with students... they just frown on it in the residents... go figure."

I shook my head.

"I don't want to limit your chanc—"

"—enough of that, now." He tipped up my chin and kissed me. "You're shook—not a surprise, given your last meeting with Jensen. We've been through all this. Now, about this dinner..."

Yes, and we'll doubtless go through it more, before we're done.

Dinner was a success, but cooking it even more so.

"I had fun with you in the kitchen," Kit said, his eyes glowing, as we sat on the sofa later that evening.

I leaned back against his arm and our eyes locked.

"Me too," I murmured, as his lips took mine.

"I'm enjoying everything we do together," he said, looking at our hands, entwined. "Maybe too much."

I gulped and bit my lip.

"Would you…" Kit said, "like to stay tonight?"

Would I?

Everything in me screamed yes, other than that little voice again… the blasted thing shook its head.

"No, positively, no," it said, emphatically.

I opened my mouth to speak and shut it again. Finally, my vocal cords worked.

"Do you think it's a good—"

"—yes, I do think it's a good idea, but until you're comfortable with it, it's a no from me, as well," he said, his voice resigned, with only a slight tensing of his jaw.

"I'm sorry," I whispered, "but—"

"—shhh," he said. "I've told you before and I'll tell you again. I'll wait for you, for as long as it takes."

My heart flooded with… warmth? Love? I nearly begged to stay.

That wouldn't do…at all.

"School starts again soon," I said, wishing my cheeks would cool under his perusal, but pigs might fly, too.

"Good, we'll see more of each other, then."

"You still want me, even if I won't sleep with you… yet?"

"If you think that's all I want from you," he shook his head, his brow furrowed, "think again. Think hard, because that's not the way I work."

I could only stare. I'd never met anyone like him. He'd been worth waiting for. I didn't want to blow this one.

KIT FOUND me in the barns just before my ICU shift ended the next evening.

"Want to go for a bite to eat after work tonight?"

"Sounds good." I glanced at my watch. "I'll be done in fifteen."

I met him in the parking lot. He pulled me to him and leaned back against the panel of his pickup.

"Well, hello to you, too," I said, after he let go of my lips.

"How was your day?" he said, as he unlocked the truck.

"Good. Plenty of horses to keep me busy. How about yours?"

He was silent for a moment, then cleared his throat and coughed.

"Ummm… I had a visit from Dean Jensen today…" Kit wasn't smiling.

An icy blast surrounded my heart and began to squeeze as I moved over into the middle of the truck beside him in silence.

"How bad was it?" I whispered.

"Bad enough. It became noticeably worse after I compared the behavior of a lecturer and a professor, each of whom had become involved in a major way with students, to a mere resident."

My breath caught in my chest and the chill around my heart raced through my body like a winter tempest.

"What…" I let out my breath and swallowed hard.

"He's decided I'm flaunting you in their faces, by going shopping."

"But we're not even sleeping together," I wailed. "It's assumed we are, clearly. I knew this would—"

"We'll work it out. Somehow. As we decided before, we'll play resident and student at the clinics, but my life does not belong to them. Period."

I sighed and took his hand. Just holding it seemed to warm me.

"We'll be all right," I said, as firmly as I could. "At least I'll be a senior now, in case that's any consolation to them."

He met my wry grin with his own, in the blue glow of the dashboard lights.

KIT WALKED down the steps into his back yard and came toward me, phone in hand.

"You'll never believe this, but we've just been asked to assist with a foaling." Kit's brows were nearly touching, as he put down the phone

"Bit late, isn't it?" I said. "It's getting tough to get a mare pregnant by October?"

"Yes, but are you hearing yourself?" He grinned.

"Yeah, I guess I'm getting over it, with all our talks." I smiled sheepishly.

"This is your chance, darlin', let's go."

"Shall I put your dogs out back while you change?"

"How do I let you talk me into this stuff?" He looked down at his muddy, grass-stained jeans and shook his head.

"It's only fair. You help me learn to do feet and teeth, it's only right I help you with your yards. You've got to admit," I gave him a twisted grin, "they needed some work."

"Yeah, well," he threw over his shoulder as he trotted up the stairs, "the dogs do most of the digging, so I don't have to."

I shook my head as the screen door slammed behind him.

Could I really do this?

I must look okay on the outside, but I was still quaking to the core.

I stood up and jerked my shirt lower over my jeans. I called the dogs and we all dragged our feet toward the entry. From long experience, the hounds knew what was coming. They looked like I'd stolen their Christmas ham when I showed them into the garage, but I was prepared. I made them all sit, then lined up pieces of kibble on the steps. On "okay", they dashed for them.

"Good dogs," I said, and closed the door. Made *me* feel better, anyway.

Somehow my jeans had stayed relatively clean, a rare occurrence, so I pulled a clean shirt from my backpack and changed in the bathroom.

"Ready to go?" he called, his keys jangling.

"As ready as I'll ever be," I mumbled, my feet getting icier by the second.

"You *will* be fine," he said, stopping me in my tracks and kissing me briefly. "I'll show you it's nothing to be afraid of."

"TAKE the next turnoff to the left," I said, just outside city limits.

A mile down the road, a small Quarter Horse stud showed against the cropped fields.

"This is it, number 79."

As we drew to a stop outside the barn, a man dashed out.

"She's in here," he yelled, and ran back inside.

"He's got her in the barn, anyway," Kit said, with a glance at the setting sun.

I nodded and helped gather the equipment we'd need, my hands moving slower than molasses in the snow.

The man trotted out of the barn again.

"You're too late. I got the foal out, but it's a good thing you come, the mare's not lookin' so good," he said, as the wave of alcoholic fumes emanating from him nearly knocked me flat.

Kit's eyes met mine and he grabbed a stethoscope and a pair of gloves. We left the rest of the equipment at the truck and bolted inside.

My breath froze in my chest and I nearly cried out at the sight of the mare lying flat out and groaning, with a tiny foal lying by her side, its head at an odd angle to the rest of its body.

Kit dropped to the ground next to the mare and glanced at her gums, then put a hand on the foal's poll and tapped the medial canthus of its eye. Nothing. Then he touched its cornea lightly, with no response whatsoever and swore beneath his breath.

"Check the mare's heart rate," Kit said, and shoved the stethoscope at me. "Her membranes are muddy and the foal's got a broken neck." He moved to her rear end, pulling on his gloves as he went.

Before he could even touch her tail, the mare groaned, stretched her legs straight out, her head back in spasm. She jerked again and again, then she was still, with only the occasional muscle spasm marring her peace. Her heartbeat was erratic until it stopped. Soon the only sounds came from the mare's legs stirring the straw as she twitched.

"I got the foal out," the man said, his chest puffed out. "It was a hard pull, had to use the tractor, but got it out."

"What was the presentation?" Kit said, his words controlled, tight.

"Presentation? Oh, like how was the foal sitting? Well, there were two feet, but it weren't coming out, so I put a rope on its leg, one or two of em, don't remember if it were one or two, an' hooked it up to the tractor when I couldn't pull it out myself. The boss is away, so I did it myself." He grinned.

I sank to the straw beside the mare's neck, stroking for all I was worth, biting my lips together to keep from screaming at the idiot. I stared at the straw, trying to slow my frantic breathing, and then the foal's hooves came into view—the perfect tiny hooves, frilly and soft at the edges. Three were clean, but the fourth... I glanced around the straw of the stall, but there was no manure anywhere, and I began to cry uncontrollably.

"Kit," I sobbed, and pointed at the hoof, covered in feces and blood.

A big engine revved outside the barn and a door slammed.

A tall, powerful-looking man strode toward the stall, his face thunderous, ham-fists clenched.

"What's going on here?" he growled, looking from the foal, to the mare, to his still-smiling barn manager leaning back in a corner, and then to Kit.

"What have you done with my daughter's mare?" His eyes shot daggers at Kit.

9

"I'm sorry sir, but—" Kit started

"—damned right you're sorry," snapped the man. "After I get through with you, you'll be sorry you ever stepped on this place."

"You're Mr. Kent?" Kit spat.

"I am," he snarled. "What are you—"

"—this mare died within one minute of our arrival. We've got one dead mare, a foal with broken neck and manure and blood on one hoof, and a drunk stableman, plus a tractor with bloody ropes tied to the back of it outside. You put it together, *sir*," Kit said, his words clipped.

I gripped his sleeve, trying to hold on as the white lights spun around my head and my legs wobbled.

"Is she dead? She was alive—" The stableman's words, and his breath, were cut short as the big man grabbed him by the throat and dragged him from the stable and outside.

I jumped to my feet and threw my arms around Kit while he gripped me so tightly I thought my ribs would crack.

"Poor, poor foal, and mare. I wonder how long she suffered," I said.

"The foal's dry, so quite some time, I imagine," he muttered into my hair.

Thudding and grunts came from outside the door and when the man returned, his fists were cut and bloody. I took one look at him, ran from the stall and slid down against the stall wall, my head clamped between my hands, but their words filtered through.

"I apologize, Doctor. I humbly apologize. When I got his message that the mare was foaling and all was well, that he had it all in hand, I didn't race right home. But I should have. Do you know why the mare died?"

"One of the foal's hooves is covered with manure and blood. I suspect when he pulled the foal... with... a... tractor," Kit bit the words out one by one, "he managed to shove one of the foal's feet through her uterus and her rectum or large colon, and the mare would have died of septic shock."

"I'm so sorry, Patience." The big man's voice was soft. There was a rustling of straw, then complete silence. "Her name was Patience, and she had more of it than any horse I'd ever met. My daughter will be... " He didn't say more for long moments. "Could you please do a post mortem? I want to know the facts."

I couldn't bear any more. I got to my feet and stumbled blindly to the truck with streaming eyes, tripping over the stableman, prone in the dirt outside the barn door. I was struggling with the door handle when Kit caught up to me. He pulled me into an embrace and held me tight against him.

"I'm so sorry, Lena." He was shaking his head, his own body quivering as much as mine. "This was not how it was supposed to go. Can you lie down in the truck for a little while? I need fifteen minutes."

I nodded and sniffed, then curled up into a ball on the back seat until he returned.

"You called it," he said, as he pulled me from the back seat and cuddled me until I stopped shaking. "As sad as it is, you got the diagnosis, first shot. The poor mare's not suffering anymore."

"Tell me this is just a bad dream, Kit—that people really don't do things like this," I whispered into his drenched shirt front.

"I wish I could," he said, "but *this* is why you need to get over your fear, so you can help prevent pointless deaths like this, by educating people, though how you'll teach a drunk, I can't say."

I cried harder, but I knew in my heart he was right.

How to make that happen remained a complete and utter mystery.

"Lena," Kit said, pulling me closer as he turned off the engine. "Earth calling Lena."

"I'm here," I murmured, and lifted my eyes to his.

"Come on, we're home."

I looked around. We were parked in Kit's driveway and his dogs had already set up a raucous howling behind the garage door.

Then he was beside me, pulling me out. My legs didn't feel like they'd carry me and I stumbled as my feet hit the pavement, but he picked me up and carried me to the doorway. He held me with one arm while he unlocked the door.

"Just a minute," he called to the dogs while he set me down on the sofa. "Stay put, I'll let out the slathering hounds, okay?"

I nodded and gave him a faint grin.

A flood of black and white, brown, and brindle dashed toward me, then separated into the two dogs and a bitch, all ingratiatingly wriggling over my knees and lap, begging for cuddles. Kit knew what I needed. I wrapped my arms around all of them as they licked any part of me they could get at and my remaining sobs became laughter by the time he returned from the kitchen with two cups of cocoa and a handful of cookies.

We shared out some cookies, then he fed them their dinner. They retired to their beds and he sat down beside me and pulled me into his lap.

"They're so loving... why can't people be like that?" I shook my head.

"Some of us are," Kit said. He kissed me, then pulled out his 104 and wiped away the remains of my tears. "I'm so sorry to have dragged you into the middle of that one, but... it can only go up from here."

"I hope so," I whispered.

"It's got me shook too, Lena," he said, burying his face in my neck. "I need to hold you tonight, as much as you need to be held."

I snuggled deeper into his chest and closed my eyes. "If only—" I started.

"Would you like to—" Kit said, speaking at the same time. We tipped our heads back and looked at each other.

"You first," he said.

"Well, I was thinking... if only I didn't have to leave your arms tonight, I might get through it," I said, and planted my face against his chest, cheeks burning.

"And I was asking if you'd like to stay here in my arms —all night." He swallowed hard.

Our eyes met, and we both slowly nodded.

"Stay right there, hold that thought. I need to sort these dogs."

He was right back and reaching for me. I put my arms around his neck and he picked me up and carried me down the hall to his room where candles flickered in the warm night breeze.

OH MY...

I swore softly beneath my breath.

What have I done?

It was the only thought in my head as we drove across town the next morning.

When I woke up, all the doors and windows in Kit's house were open and Grateful Dead echoed down the hall at a tremendous volume. I shook my head and sat up.

I slept through that? I must've been wiped.

Kit was friendly, when I found him in the kitchen, but a wall that hadn't been there in months stood solidly between us.

"I have to head off to the clinics, I'll see you later," he said, with a brief peck on the cheek.

"Ummm, Kit," I said, biting my lip, "My truck's at the clinics."

He swallowed hard.

"Best get your stuff, I'll drop you by there."

If this was keeping it "cool at school", I wondered what we'd do for a finale.

Our talk on the way in was... pedestrian at best, but we both survived, and breathed a collective sigh of relief when we reached my vehicle in the employee parking lot, with no one in sight.

"Thank you for last night," I murmured, as I unbuckled myself from the passenger seat.

"Lena," he said, low, and I looked up to see him reaching for my hand.

I gave it, and stood, biting my lip, looking at our conjoined hands.

"It'll be all right. There *will* be little hiccups, but we'll be okay."

I took a deep breath and held it.

"Okay. I hope so," I said, and kissed his knuckles. "Have a good day, Kit, I will... too."

"HI JESS, WELCOME BACK," I said, wrapping my arms around her in a bearhug after she stepped through our doorway later that day.

"Hi, missed ya," she said, returning the hug with a big smile, then turned to Tamarah. "Hiya, I hope Lena's behaved while I was gone."

Tamarah looked at me sideways from her spot on the sofa.

"I know nothing," she said, holding up her hands, "but welcome back, Jess."

Jess swore under her breath when she spied the half-eaten tub of chocolate gelato on the table, a big spoon sticking out of it.

"Can't I even leave you on your own for the summer?"

"Apparently not," I mumbled.

"You only do this after a heinous breakup." Jess shook her head and hugged me again.

"Well this is infinitely worse," I said, to my boots. "Falling for a resident, sleeping with him, and—oh, no," I flicked a glance at the round paper container on the table and squeezed my eyes shut, "half a tub of gelato, which'll go straight to my butt."

"KIT, we've been going out away from town, so we don't have any more meetups like we did with the Jensens," I said to him, a few weeks later, with a shudder, then went on in a rush, "but I wanted to invite you to the vet school senior Christmas dinner and dance. It'll be a lot of fun—it's on a riverboat on the Delta." I bit my lip. I wanted to go with him, despite my gut feeling that it wasn't the best idea I'd ever had.

He froze, a thousand emotions flitting across his face, then he gulped and reached out to take my hand.

"I'd—I'd like that." His eyes warmed, but with a flicker of —something.

"Are you sure it's worth it? Going public with the hierarchy?"

"It'll... be okay." He kissed me. "You're worth it. If they don't want me because I want you, well, then, maybe I'll just... apply somewhere else..." he said, but he shuffled his feet and the fingers of the hand not holding mine toyed with his pager like a pacifier.

I let out the breath I didn't know I'd been holding. I still wasn't convinced, but my face warmed as he pulled me close, rested his chin on top of my head, and just held me. I didn't want it to ever end.

"You know," he said, "I could get used to this—"

—*beep, beep, beep, beep.*

"Damn," I muttered. "I used to love that thing."

He looked at me sideways and I managed a grin as he headed for the phone.

I truly used to love pagers, but... they were starting to niggle a bit—and it wasn't the pagers' fault. It was like there was no one else on the planet other than the person on the other end of that pager—and the scary thing was, he'd never looked at me with that same glow.

I'm sure I'll get over it. It's our life, remember?

—*BEEP, beep, beep, beep.*

The pager again. No doubt about it, it was starting to make me crazy.

Or was that more crazy?

"Sometimes I wish you'd just take that off," I said, gritting my teeth to keep from scowling.

"I thought you liked the pager," he said, lifting a brow.

"You're not on call tonight, though, are you?"

That thin veil lately present between us thickened to the consistency of plywood.

"No," he said, his jaw tight. "But someone may want to get hold of me."

I took a deep breath, considering how much to say. A spate of lightning storms had meant a run of injured horses and the clinics were full to overflowing. For the past three weeks, he hadn't finished before midnight and had started each day by six. I'd been working extra shifts and still had my treatments to do as well in my rotations, now that school had begun. Irritable didn't begin to define us. We were shattered.

"Kit, we've been killing ourselves and we finally have a day off."

"What's wrong with being available for my clients and patients?" he snapped.

"We're off today. Others are covering… and whenever that pager goes… it's like you want to be as far away from me as you can get."

"Now you're just getting bitchy," he said. "I thought you liked being a veterinarian, or at least the *thought* of being a veterinarian, and helping animals."

"I do, it's just that… I'm afraid when that pager goes… you might not return," I finished on a whisper.

"What is it, really?" he growled.

It was a long time before I spoke.

"Truthfully? I'm afraid I'll never be as important to you as... your work."

"Now you're just being silly," he mumbled, a little hesitantly. "There are animals out there that need us. When the pager goes, we go," he said. "Have a good night. I'm off."

He didn't even ask if I wanted to go.

It looked like a collision course, with no end in sight. I shivered at the thought of our planned trip up north. How would that go?

10

"Your wish is my command, milady." Kit swept me a bow, his pager in hand, a few weeks later, then set the little black and silver demon in its storage slot at the teaching hospital. "And there it will stay for the next—" he clutched at his neck and staggered toward the door, "—six-six-sixty hours," he said, "if it kills me."

I couldn't help laughing as I followed him out the door, headed for the freedom of a weekend away.

"You ready to rock?" he said.

"Everything's in the back of your pickup."

"I feel naked," he said, grabbing at his belt, where his pager usually sat.

"You look fine." I gave him a slow smile.

Things had improved between us as the caseload diminished back to its normal dull roar. We still kept "us" under wraps at the clinics, but things were working out beautifully outside of the university. We even found time to do some feet and teeth. Even I could see my technique was improving, and for that, I would be eternally grateful to my Kit.

"THE WEEKEND'S BEEN MAGICAL, thanks for asking me along, Kit," I said, as we headed home on Sunday afternoon. "Just the right combination of fun, talks for the horse groups, and visits to your favorite old clients."

"So, what did you learn?" He smiled and took my hand.

"Nuances of presenting to groups, how to dehorn a seven-year old buck—that was by no means a simple procedure. More importantly, though, I got to see what truly devoted clients look like. My devotion to my own equine vet when I was a girl bordered on hero worship, and it was wonderful to see what you meant to them, way out there in the boonies."

"I sure love this little town," Kit said, with a glance back at the last signs of habitation as we drove away through the redwoods.

"It's pretty special and the people are great, but this is a *big* town," I said.

He blinked.

"Oh yeah, you came from La Honda. It's *teeny.*"

"Just the way I like it," I said, with a grin. "Five hundred people and that's on a busy day."

"Hey, what do you say we stop at the river for a swim? It's just a little way along from here."

"You know me, this fish'll always swim." I grinned.

"I think it's time," Kit said, his voice level and devoid of emotion, "we started working on that foaling problem of yours again, after our last disastrous episode. Foaling season will be here sooner than you think."

He looked across at me as I began sliding down in my seat.

"And don't check out on me. I have a captive audience for the next several hours," he said, with a lascivious grin.

I nodded, but my guts tensed.

"There's more to this... more fears," he continued. "I don't think it was losing that first mare at all, though it probably compounded it."

"I've been thinking about it a lot, too, and I don't either..."

"You don't? Do tell."

"I've always been," I took a deep breath and fiddled with my seatbelt, "driven to do better, try harder. All my mother ever said was to do my best, and that I could do anything I wanted if I was willing to make it happen. I thought I was driven by the desire to never be left in my mom's situation when my father walked up to us in a room full of other people and tossed a keychain with a yellow boat floatie onto the table before us—for his new houseboat. Mom had no formal education and no job skills other than being a great parent, and she struggled."

"Seriously? That was your introduction to his move out of your life?"

I swallowed hard and nodded.

"To this day, sighting one of those yellow floaties on someone's keychain makes my chest feel like it's caving in. But I think it was before that, even. I just don't know."

"Were you as driven before that?"

"I think so, but I'll ask my mom when she gets back from New Zealand."

"Does she live there?"

"No, she's mountain biking over there with my stepdad."

"Wow, she must be young."

"Young at heart, and gutsy, to boot."

"I see where you got it, then," he said, with a chuckle.

"Unlike mom, however, I have more guts than brains."

"You have plenty of both—don't sell yourself short. You seem pretty insecure about personal things, though... your classmates... and me, for example."

"I don't know where it comes from, I mean, I had a wonderful childhood, loving parents, no abuse, so?"

"Can't help with your past, but we can work with the here and now. So how about we talk about foaling… just a little, every day, and we'll break through it," Kit said, as he pulled off the road and onto a dirt track. He stopped the truck and came around to open my door.

I inhaled until my ribs wanted to collapse in on themselves and looked up at him. His green eyes were nearly black now as they met mine.

I nodded, yes, and our lips met.

11

How could anything be wrong when it felt so right?

Soft lamplight glittering off polished brass fittings created a warm refuge from the storm howling outside as the Sacramento Delta paddle wheeler rocked gently at her moorings. Despite the weather, the Christmas party was fully attended and dinner had been exquisite.

Holding my hands, Kit gazed at me and reached down for a kiss. His beautiful eyes glowed. I could almost ignore the sideways glances from the other students and faculty as we walked, hand in hand, to the punch bowl. Kit must've seen the looks, too, for he pulled me closer to his side.

I was a fairy queen for the night in my delicately flowered soft pink Lanz dress, with a thousand tiny buttons from my nape to my tailbone, puffed sleeves and a smooth princess line, ending in a deep V over my abdomen.

And Kit could dance. We waltzed, floating around the dance floor, my taffeta and net petticoats peeking from beneath my skirts as we swirled.

"Tonight is so perfect," I whispered to him.

"It's easily the highlight of the past five years for me," he said, and pulled me closer in his arms.

There's something about a man who can lead you around the floor in a waltz. If I were a heroine in a Regency novel, "swooning" would have been high on the agenda. I smiled.

"What?" His brow furrowed.

"You'll laugh."

"Try m—"

—*beep, beep, beep, beep.*

I blinked. Not really. I shook my head at his joke, with a mischievous grin.

He looked at me and winced.

"But you're not on call," I said, my smile melting.

"Well… I wasn't, but… Melissa wanted to go back home for the—"

"—let's go," I said, with a sigh, biting back the words threatening to escape. It was pointless.

"You wait here, I'm sure it'll be nothing," he said, with a squeeze of his fingers, and bolted.

"Dumped again, princess?" came a voice from behind me that turned my blood to ice. "And by a resident? Aren't you a little out of your class? He's stooping a bit low—feed rooms, I hear?" Gareth seemed to have a homing device for my moments of weakness or despair. I gritted my teeth and held my body rigid. I no longer had to give him the time of day. His footsteps sauntered away and I could breathe again.

Maybe I am reaching too high.

I tried to ignore the little voice, but it niggled as I gazed out through the fat droplets pelting the porthole in the heavy gusts of wind.

I lifted my head to find Kit among the throng of partygoers, seeing them as through a pane of glass. I finally spotted him, wending his way back.

Professor Gates tapped him on the shoulder as he passed

and Kit paused, then turned back to face him. I couldn't see Kit's face, but the professor's showed clearly—and it couldn't have been a pleasant conversation. His moustache jerked as he spoke in staccato fashion, then he swung back to his group of residents and fellow professors.

My lungs drained and I was powerless to fill them as I looked away and gripped the doorway for support. My legs felt insufficient to the task.

Tears again? This had to stop.

Two hands slid around my waist and I froze, but then Kit's scent came to me, his lips on my neck.

"Miss me much?"

"Don't you know it," I said, with fervor, as the tension from Gareth's jibes dissipated. Desiring, but fearing, to ask about Professor Gates, I held my peace.

Kit opened his mouth against the nape of my neck and then shut it again. Finally, he inhaled sharply and turned me in his arms.

"It's a foaling."

I swallowed hard, my guts clenching, but then I blinked.

"Another out-of-season foal?"

"Crazy, eh?" Kit shook his head. "How the heck she got pregnant in the middle of the winter, I'll never know. Will you come?"

I winced and held my breath.

"If you'd rather stay for the party, I can get James to take you home—the night's young yet." He gave a wistful glance at the couples on the polished dance floor.

I didn't want to leave his side, but a *foaling*?

"Lena, you're white as a sheet. Come on, we've been talking about all this."

A rush of hopelessness filled me. This man could never be mine. I'd never be good enough or devoted enough to get past the fear and be a good partner for him. He couldn't really want to be with me—and to take me to a foaling after the last one? I don't think I could take it.

"I'm all right," I said. I set my jaw as my legs wobbled, knuckles ivory on the bannister.

"Hey, Allen," Gareth's voice cut between us, "you're hogging all the pretty girls." He stumbled up beside us and I shrank from his touch when he gripped the railing close beside me.

"Haven't you already graduated?" Kit said, his voice edgy. "What are you doing back here?"

"Sure have, and I'm here with a date," Gareth said, smirking. "Did I ever tell you, Doc," he spoke to Kit, but his eyes were on me as he leered, "how good in bed she—"

"—I think you've had enough to drink, Barnett, don't you?" Kit cut in, his voice low and sharp.

Gareth went on like he hadn't heard, his gaze fixed on my bodice, and then his hands were on my breasts, his fingers tangling in my hair.

With a yank of my hair, Gareth's hands disappeared, and I think he shouted. Then came a crash of metal and glass as I cringed beside the railing, eyes squeezed shut, tears hot on my cheeks. Just the sound of his voice turned me to stone, but his touch—it brought back the pain, the anger. Someone was crying—I think it was me—and I focused on sucking oxygen in and letting it out as my world began to right itself again. And then Kit was there, holding me like he'd never let go.

"I won't leave you behind," he murmured into my ear. "Is anyone at your house?"

"N-n-no," I managed, between sobs, his warm chest a beacon in the darkness, and I clung like a limpet.

"Come on, he's not getting another go at you, even if he could. You're coming with me."

"To a foaling?" It came out as a strangled cry. There wasn't even room in my mind to wonder what had happened to

Gareth, but it couldn't have been more than he deserved, anyway.

Kit took one look at my face and gripped my hands so hard his fists turned white, the parts that weren't already red-tinged.

"Stay with me, Lena, we'll work it out. Let's go." He released one hand and strode off toward the coat check, pulling me in his wake.

On my four inch heels, I stumbled blindly beside him into a wind that would've knocked me flat if I hadn't been glued to his side. The rain had abated, but water still flew horizontally off trees and railings as we walked down the gangplank.

"That guy is a jerk, but there's more to this. What was all that about?" he said, when we were out in the parking lot.

Dragging gulps of the cold delta night air into my lungs restored my blood pressure, if not my equanimity, while I scrambled for an answer that didn't sound completely nuts.

"I don't do drunk people," I said.

He didn't answer for a moment. Stupid, he was not, and I kicked myself for not telling him before.

"What happened between the two of you?" he said, as he led me along the sidewalk.

"Happened?"

"You and Gareth were an item—what changed that?"

I considered. What sort of a fool stays in that sort of a relationship? He'd think I was an idiot—and he wouldn't be far wrong. I gritted my teeth.

"Ummm—we didn't get on."

He gripped my hand tighter and stopped, so I had to turn and face him under a streetlight.

"Tell me about it," his voice was cold and calm, but the honed steel edge beneath was unmistakable.

"He got rough when he'd had a few too many." I turned

my face up to him and bit my lip. "I'm sorry, I should have told you about him... and me, but it's long past."

"Damn glad to hear that," he growled, "the past part, anyway." His eyes narrowed and a tic started up in his jaw. He glanced back toward the floating party boat and tensed, then took a deep breath.

"Knew it didn't feel right, leaving you there," he murmured, and squeezed my hand as I nodded.

"Thank you, Kit." I meant it with all my heart.

"No problem." He kissed me on the forehead. "I could drop you home, but you don't look so good." He frowned and reconsidered. "Well, you look like a princess, but—"

"—I know what you mean." I smiled at him through my tears. "I felt like one back there, in your arms."

He smiled and grunted, a seemingly appropriate male response to such a statement, then kissed me again, in a way that left no doubt of his feelings.

"Despite whatever happened in the past," Kit said, "you're still a princess to me... and I don't want to drop you home alone. You can come with me."

I could only stare at his back as he pulled me along.

He stopped and looked back at me.

"Please, Lena? Let's get you over this foaling thing." He squeezed my hand. "It's just another procedure, like a dog spay or a horse castration."

Damn me if I could see straight to put my feet in a line and walk. I gripped his hand as my guts churned and I doubled over.

"What is it?"

I couldn't answer and huddled within myself. "I can't help with a foaling," I whispered.

He blinked, then frowned.

"I just can't," I wailed, my respiratory rate hitting top level.

"Too pink to get your hands dirty?" he bit out. That got me, and my temper flared.

"Of course not," I growled. I hated the thought of girlie-pink—that was for my sister—and here I was, dressed in it. I had to smile, despite myself.

"Sorry, that was the wrong thing to say," Kit looked at his boots, "but really, they don't all die, and we need to go. If you really aren't willing, you can sit in the car. At least I'll know you're safe."

"I'm not really dressed for an emergency in the rain." I looked down at the lace and frills of my dress, flapping in the wind.

I held my breath while he unlocked the door and reached inside.

"Your scrubs and boots, milady," Kit said.

"Couldn't stretch to a jacket, could you?" I managed.

"Yes," he made a face, "but they've been down behind the seat for quite some time, so I can't guarantee their condition. They're probably doggy."

"Beggars can't be choosers," I said, then remembered the buttons. Tamarah had fastened me into this dress. Given enough time, I could get out of it, but in a hurry... I started, but trying to reach behind my back in the icy breeze wasn't working. With everything else tonight, I was nearly in tears with frustration.

"Shhh, I'll help," Kit murmured from behind me, in the tone he used with frightened horses. His nimble fingers had them undone in seconds as the wind whistled around the side of the cab and the rain began again in earnest. His warm breath and the flutter of a kiss on my nape contrasted sharply with the breeze cutting down my front.

I turned toward him and stood on tiptoe to kiss him lightly on the lips.

"Dress yourself." He handed me a set of scrubs, his eyes

sparkling in the light of a streetlamp. "You're too tempting like this. Not quite the situation I'd envisaged for tonight, but as you say, beggars can't be choosers. Away you go," he said.

I dashed around to the passenger side and pulled on Kit's scrub pants. I had to laugh as I bent to roll up the extra foot of length. Although this side of the vehicle was out of the worst of the weather, wind still whipped through the thin cotton scrub pants and up my dress. I shivered harder, my teeth already chattering. The yards of skirt slid off over my head, then the ruffly petticoat, and finally I could dive into the shirt. At least that fit. With the jacket over it, I smelled a bit like a wet sheep, but a toasty-warm one.

"You about ready out there?" Kit called, already in the driver's seat.

I gripped the truck door, chewing the inside of my cheeks, then climbed in.

"Righto, Lena, let's talk this through."

"Kit, first... please, I saw Professor Gates talking with you."

He froze and his face fell.

"What did he say? He looked pretty angry."

"Yes," he took a deep breath, "he was."

"About us?"

"It doesn't matter, and I told him so."

"You can't just give it up, all you've worked for... for a relationship."

"This is you and me we're talking about, Lena. Don't you want it?" His jaw bulged with tension.

"More than anything, but, but..." I stuttered.

"But what? It's my decision how I reach my goals. Can't you trust me with that? You, we, are important to me. Faculty members have their little rules, but they break them themselves. Since I'm a lowly resident, they think they can dictate my personal life, and... they can't. And they don't like it."

I could only stare. I wish I felt I deserved this kind of loyalty, but maybe I could start to believe.

"Anyway, that's sorted. I told him... but... " Kit hesitated, "Gates just dropped a bombshell."

I gripped my hands together and moved closer.

"You know Professor Salandro? The one pioneering neurosurgery in horses?"

"From Sweden?" Kit nodded.

"Well, he's coming for a sabbatical the year after next... when I was hoping to be on my tenure track position... here."

"Oh, no, Kit." I tried to swallow the rock in my throat.

"I want to work with Professor Salandro more than anyone else in the world. Gates knows it, and he's using that as bait."

I sank back against the seat and shut my eyes. *How* could I let him choose me and lose this opportunity?

"Let me make my own decisions, okay?" Kit said and reached for my hand.

I swallowed hard and sat up again.

"And... there's one other thing," I said, "but I think you've sorted it."

"What have I sorted?" He frowned at the windscreen. "Gareth spat something about our playing around in feed rooms. One of his friends in my class on treatment crew must have told him... and he must've told the dean."

"Come to think of it, he just mentioned that. I was nearly done with him, but after he gave me that little bit of information, I dealt with that, too."

I blinked and opened my mouth, but nothing came out.

"Back to tonight. We're going to a foaling and you can, and will, handle it. We'll do it together and you'll be a star."

"I guess I can always wait tables again, after I get expelled," I whispered, my world bottoming out.

"I'll be there," he said firmly, and reached across the cab to take my hand. "You're too far away. Move that junk, will you?

There's a box in back." He nodded at the towels, patient record forms, a stethoscope, and… a dog collar?

I picked up the pile and half-climbed over the seat to dump it beside the heap of pink that was my dress, then buckled up again.

"Come on over here." He patted the seat beside him. "We need to figure this out."

"Nothing we can do," I hissed. "I told you before, I can't do them. I make things die."

"Not tonight, you won't. If we can't foal the mare, the vet school is just down the road. Let's talk about treatment of dystocia. We'll see how awake you were during my lecture."

"I'd be lucky to remember anything," I said, my face heating, "once the pretty foal pictures finished and the gritty bits started."

"It'll be a long drive in this," Kit shouted, as the heavens opened up and the deluge pounding on the roof of the truck threatened to wipe out the sound of his voice, "so we have plenty of time." He switched the wipers to fast. "So, what can you recall? How about starting at the beginning?"

I took a deep breath to settle myself and began.

"THAT HOUSE LOOKS AWFULLY DARK." With another twinge of anxiety as we drove into the yard, I rechecked the house number Kit had written down.

"Hopefully the mare's in that nice, dry barn," he said, nodding at the massive structure beside the house.

"With big fluffy towels and buckets of hot water," I said, letting a grin escape. I truly hoped so as I glanced at the windshield wipers still racing along on max. The blades nearly kept pace with my heart, but were only barely clearing the glass in the tempest we'd been driving through for the past hour.

"I'm not sure where the owner is," Kit said, looking around at the unlit house and barn. One big barn door was open, so we pulled the truck inside and hopped out. "Let's get out what you'll need," he said. "This foaling's yours."

I shuddered, my guts making mincemeat of the fine dinner we'd just eaten on the riverboat, and shook my head. It seemed a year ago we'd left the party. I gave thanks Kit would be there to keep me in one piece. There was no way I could do this on my own.

"There aren't any horses in the barn—I'm not sure what's up." Kit shook his head after he'd found the light switch. "I hope we got the address right."

My hands trembled as I assembled foaling gowns, syringes, needles, drugs, gloves, disinfectant, and lube, then dumped them into several buckets. I shuddered and turned my face away from the embryotome and embryotomy wire. I just couldn't go there. Like Kit said, the mare could go to the university.

The sound of feet splashing through puddles came to me over the din of the raindrops pelting the barn's steel roof. I spun to see a bedraggled, dripping teenager stumble in through the doorway.

"Dr. Allen?" she said, terror sharp in her voice. I froze in my tracks, remembering.

"Yes, and Lena, a veterinary student. Are you Stacey?"

"Yep, you...found us." She leaned over and braced her hands on her knees to get her breath. "I'm sorry," she panted, between her words, "but the mare's up on the... other side of the... river. She's not due... yet, and the river came up. I didn't have anyone to help me... get her across after it... started rising."

"It's okay." Kit ducked down to her height and put his

hands on her shoulders. "We can go to wherever she is. Can we drive there?"

"No," she winced, "you'll have to... cross the swing bridge. You'll never... make it around to the other one in this weather... too steep and too... slippery."

"Okay, we've nearly got everything we need," he said, rechecking the buckets.

As I listened to her, my anxiety level rose by the second, and I could barely think straight.

"Don't you need a jacket?" Kit said, as the girl stood shivering in her dripping western shirt, the fabric nearly as shiny with water as her pearl snaps.

"Good idea," she said, and twisted around, heading for a door at the back of the barn.

"Oh, Kit," I gripped his jacket, "she's about the same age as I was..." Every part of my body shook and I was close to snapping.

"Hold on, Lena," he said, through gritted teeth. "We're not going to lose this mare, I promise. Breathe. The last thing that girl needs is you flipping out."

I focused with everything I had in me. By the time she returned, wearing a dry shirt and a waterproof jacket, I'd composed myself into some semblance of a confident professional. With any luck, the girl wouldn't see my tumbling emotions, barely hidden beneath the surface.

"Where's your family? Are you all alone here?" Kit asked.

I gritted my teeth to keep from speaking.

"Yes." Stacey bit her trembling lip. "I told them I could take care of everything. Goldie isn't due for three more weeks, so I told them to go on the vacation they've been needing... I was so sure I could take care of... everything." This last at a whisper as tears began to roll. "And this mare, Goldie, short for Clapton's Gold..." she gulped, "is my good show horse... and the best cuttin' horse Daddy ever had. Can you save her,

Dr. Allen? I'd like the foal, but I want Goldie to live more than anything in this world."

He took a deep breath and swallowed hard.

"I'll do my best, Stacey, and we have Lena here to help us too. She's knowledgeable and a good hand with a horse."

"My friend's mom had you out to see her horse, Dr. Allen, and my Mom said that my *friend's* mom thinks the sun shines out of your... oh." She stopped, her mouth open, then she snapped it shut and took a deep breath. "She said you're... the most amazing vet. I know you can save her."

Kit and I struggled for composure, but he mastered it first. I ducked behind him until I could keep a straight face, my fears forgotten for a moment.

"So where is the mare?" he said, as the girl led us into the storm.

"She's across the river, up there," she shouted, and pointed to a field on the other side of the high bank of a river... half a mile away.

I gulped and closed my eyes, then set my buckets down to tighten the cord on my hood against the pelting rain, but it was too late. Water was already running down my neck in rivulets.

Kit stopped and did the same, then took one of my buckets in addition to his own, squeezed my hand, and we raced after the fleeing girl.

Even in the semi-darkness between flashes of lightning, the suspension bridge looked more and more rickety as we neared it. The closer we got to the horse laboring somewhere ahead, the harder it was to suck air into my lungs and I started to hyperventilate again.

"Is the bridge safe, Stacey?" Kit's shout was barely audible over the wind.

"Sure is, I use it all the time. The boards are a little slippery when it's wet, but it'll be fine," she yelled, as she raced across it.

"I'm not keen on the look of that bridge in this wind," Kit yelled to me. "I'm going to leave the lube bottle and one of these buckets here so I have a free hand. You okay?"

I looked at the span from the corners of my eyes. My stomach, unsettled before, positively flipped over.

"Yes," I squeaked, shaking. My breath caught in my chest as I took my first step onto it, then stretched to reach over a gap where several boards must have once been bolted in place. The homemade wooden platforms on the banks, the far side a good fifteen feet higher than the near one, creaked hideously in the gale as the bridge swayed.

"Excellent," Kit said, from behind her. "That higher bank will cut some of the wind for us. Do you think you can—"

My brains collided with my emotions. Gripping my bucket with one hand, I let go of the handrail to grab Kit's jacket with the other, like a crazy thing.

"I can't do it," I said, "I just can't... she... she reminds me too much of me—I was that age when it all happened, and the storm—it's all just the same—I can't be there and let her down. I just can't. I'm sorry Kit, but I can't."

He turned, fury and pity warring on his face. Fury won.

"Suck it up, girl," Kit shouted over the gale and the creaking of the wildly-swinging bridge. "Whatever else is going on in your life, you can't be that selfish—you've got a horse out there that needs you. Get on with it. We'll do it together. Here, I found some of those soft foaling ropes. Shove them inside your jacket, there's no more room in the buckets."

A bit of anger helped quell my fear as I girded up my loins and started for the far shore.

"Can you take this bucket, too?" he yelled after me. "I'm going back for the other one and the lube. Be there in just a sec." He shoved the cold metal at me and spun in the other direction, skidded to a halt, turned back and raced toward me. He kissed me on the mouth, hard. "You can do it. I'll be right beside you, now go," he said, more gently, and wiped at the tears and the rain running down my face.

I managed a hint of a smile for him, blindly grabbing for the handle as I looked at him, then stumbled on forward over the bridge as he trotted away. A board gave way beneath my boot with a sickening lurch and my foot slipped between its two neighbors, but I somehow grabbed the rope hand rails and the buckets in the same hands and ripped my foot out, grinding my teeth together.

"Suck it up, indeed," I growled. "I'll get to that mare if it kills me."

Only the wind answered, as I struggled toward the far shore

"Selfish, eh?" My anger fought against my fear and I blinked as the penny dropped. It *was* selfish, having hysterics over something that happened so long ago, something I was never trained to do. It didn't take away the fear, but it strengthened my resolve. I took a deep breath and staggered on.

I was nearly to the far anchoring platform when a rogue gust of wind caught the already-swaying bridge and jerked it hard enough to knock Kit's bucket from my hand and send it tumbling to the dark, boiling flood below.

"Nooooo," I yelled, grabbing for the bucket, but it was gone. I was scrabbling for the handrail ropes again, when the foot boards disappeared completely from beneath my feet. The handrails followed and we dropped like a stone in a downward arc. I lunged and somehow caught the ropes as they swung toward the far wall and held on for dear life while the foaming water raged, far too close, beneath my feet.

12

"K *it!*" I screamed, as my head and body slammed against the sheer rock wall beneath the bridge anchor.

I clung to the slippery ropes and shook my head, trying to clear it, while bright lights spun around me and we swung to a halt a yard and a half from the cliff face. A weight cut sharp into one arm as I gripped the lifelines. My mouth dropped open at the sight of the full bucket, against all odds, still hanging from arm. I glanced up into the pouring rain. My scrap of bridge was still attached to the platform's extension out over the river, but the span must've broken somewhere behind me.

My arms shook as I took in the sheer granite wall, its black and gray surface glittering in a stray patch of moonlight. I managed to get a grip with my feet on one of the remaining walkway planks, now situated like a decrepit ladder, and flung the bucket as hard as I could, up and over the edge of the bank, praying I didn't hit Stacey. Nothing came back to smack me on the head, giving me hope that the gear had made it up to the top. I glanced again at the rock wall before me and shook my head, my mouth drying at the mere thought. I wasn't ascending that without my climbing gear. Taking a firmer grip on the ropes, I twisted around to see what had become of Kit.

My blood ran cold at the sight of Kit's side of the span, rattling and bouncing parallel to the swollen river, partly in and partly out of the flood. Just downriver, a flailing figure that could only be Kit was being swept away, but at least he was nearing the far bank.

At the sight of a massive log heading straight for Kit, my breath lodged in my chest, then I gasped, like a fish out of water.

"Look out, Kit!" I screamed, knowing he surely couldn't hear me. I could do nothing for him unless I let go and joined him in the surging, dark water—and then we'd both probably drown, leaving no one to help Stacey and her struggling mare.

No choice.

I needed to get up the bank. Dangling in the air above the river was no help to anyone, and who knew how long my ropes would hold.

Inch by screaming inch, with plenty of false starts and slips, I clambered my way up, arms burning with the effort. It'd been far too long since my rock climbing days. My first peek over the top showed Stacey racing towards me. She dragged me over the top and away from the edge, then hugged me.

"Are you okay? I saw the bridge go, I'm so sorry!" She looked around me and down the bank, then spun back.

Where's Dr Allen?" she shrieked, her voice edging on hysteria.

Heart in my throat, I pointed across the dark waters, then breathed a sigh of relief at the sight of his figure, still very much alive, nearing the far shore.

"His half of the bridge landed in the water," I said, my voice as shaky as the rest of me. "I hope he can get out."

Stacey looked up and down the river.

"We can't help him from here and there's no use three of us drowning," she whispered. "He's big and strong. We just have to believe he'll make it out."

I nodded, my heart clenching.

Stacey sounded more confident than she looked. She grabbed my hand as Kit reached the far shore and clambered out. He struggled back along the river toward us and raised his face, glowing white in the darkness. He shouted something, but we couldn't hear it for the rushing of the water.

"Again?" I yelled, and froze to listen.

His voice came faintly on the breeze: "You'll have to do it yourself, Lena. You can do it, I know you can."

"Oh no, I can't," I screamed, then my breath clutched in my throat. Somehow, even in the slashing rain, my mouth felt like I'd been stranded in the desert for a week.

"You'll have to," he called back. "You can do it."

I shrank away from him, from the river, and from the bucket, its contents scattered over the bank before me.

"Come on," yelled Stacey. "You can do it. If Dr Allen thinks you can, you can. Let's go!"

"Is there any way across the river other than this?" I shouted above the gale, biting my lip.

"There is, but he'll never find it. You'll have to do it on your own. I believe in you." Her knuckles were white as she gripped the sides of her jacket.

A thousand thoughts raced through my mind as I flicked a glance at Stacey and my heart just stopped. My feet froze to the ground, like they'd been stuck in concrete.

"You can do this." Stacey grabbed my hand. "You may not be a vet yet, but you know what to do. If Dr. Allen thinks you do, you do. I believe in him, and I believe in you." Her little jaw was set, her eyes steely.

Dr. Allen… Kit

I forced myself to focus. He was out of the water and alive. He'd prepared me. I gulped for air and gripped my shaking hands together.

I shook my head at myself. If Stacey, a teenager with her beloved horse's life on the line, could hold her hysteria in check, I could certainly do the same. I couldn't let her have the same experience I'd had. I *did* know how. I *did* have the knowledge. I just had to get over myself. Isn't that what people say? Feel the fear and do it anyway? I swallowed it and straightened my spine. I was given the gift of this knowledge. Now wasn't the time to waste it.

With one last wistful look over my shoulder through the seething downpour, I scrambled to gather the contents of the bucket I'd flung up onto the bank, then gear in hand, raced up the hill after Stacey. I dropped to a walk as we approached, speaking calmly to the laboring mare.

HER GUMS WERE PINK, but not overly red. With my stethoscope, I listened to her heart and lungs.

"Her heart's a bit fast, but normal for a mare in labor," I said, as I walked back to her rear end. Pulling a bandage from my pocket, I bandaged her tail to keep it out of the way. "Is there any clean water nearby?"

"Already here." Stacey's worry showed through her eyes, even past her forced smile. She reached for a ten-gallon bucket and lugged it to me.

"Well done," I murmured, lining my empty bucket with a clean garbage can liner as she pried off the lid, then poured water into my bucket. "It's warm, even." I grinned at her, and squirted some iodine into the water.

"You want some cotton in that bucket?"

"Yes, please," I said, as I cleaned the mud off my hands,

then wiped the mare's perineum with the disinfectant-soaked cotton.

I reached for the foaling gown, then realized it was probably halfway to San Francisco by now. Turning an OB sleeve inside out, I blew into it, then put it on.

"Why'd you turn that glove?".

"Puts the seams inside, less likelihood of cutting her," I said, as I lubed up my arm. "I'm thankful we have even this little bottle of lube," I said, and gulped. "Kit was going back for the big one. Guess we'll do without it."

The girl's face fell.

I'd best shut up. Stacey was already white as a ghost.

I almost chuckled as I caught myself wishing for something dry to lie on. I couldn't get much grubbier or wetter anyway. I gritted my teeth, dropped to the muddy grass, and slipped my gloved fingers into the straining mare.

Warm tissues greeted my icy fingers, and then my arm, as I reached inside her. Just inside the vulva, my hand enveloped two tiny hooves, the rubbery, frilled eponychium on their edges soft when I touched them. I reached a little further and stilled, feeling for a pulse, and my heart began to glow.

"The foal's alive," I said.

Stacey gave a little yelp and stroked Goldie as I slid my arm out again for more lubricant, wishing for a dosing syringe to instill more inside her. I reached in further, seeking, praying for a nose, but all I found was the wide expanse of the foal's chest before me. Stretching a bit, I felt the side of a neck and froze.

Not another wry neck. Please, not another one.

"What is it?"

I opened my eyes to see Stacey staring intently at me.

Oh cripes, I must *control my face.*

"The foal's head is back," I said. "Let me look a little further."

My mind raced. This couldn't be happening, not again. Tears burned hot down my cheeks and I wiped them away with my ungloved hand. I didn't have what I needed to do a cesarean here, and without it, if this was a wry neck, this foal wasn't coming out. I took a deep breath and shoved my arm back in to give me time to think.

The mare was lying on a hill with her rear end downwards, not nearly far enough from the river to make me happy, but thankfully, she wasn't that big—probably just under fifteen hands.

"Do you have any idea how long she's been in labor?" I asked. By the looks of her muddy coat, she'd been up and down for quite some time.

"She was fine when I checked her this morning," Stacey bit her lip, "but I was out all afternoon. She's not due for another few weeks, or I'd have had her down by the house," Stacey said, with a sob, as tears started rolling down her cheeks.

I could barely get my fingers in far enough to feel up the foal's neck, so I braced my flat of my hand against its little chest and pushed to see if I could repulse the baby and give me more room to work. Perhaps it wasn't a wry neck at all, just a head-back presentation? My heart leapt and I wedged my feet in the slippery grass and heaved with all my strength.

The foal never budged.

Goldie had been lying still, but now she began to push with a vengeance.

"Oh my...," I swore softly and held my breath as my arm was crushed against the sharp brim of the mare's pelvis. No option of pulling my arm out while she was bearing down. I waited, gritting my teeth, praying she'd stop soon.

"Stacey," I said softly, but still aiming to be heard over the raindrops spattering on the buckets, "did you find a little bottle with the syringes and needles? There should have been some local anesthetic in that bucket."

"Syringes and needle, yes, but no bottle."

I let out the breath I didn't know I've been holding.

No epidural, then.

The slope wasn't helping us here, but maybe...

It was worth a try.

"We're going to have to turn her around," I said, my heart surging. "The foal's head is back, which is why it's not out yet, but with Goldie's head facing up the hill, the weight of her guts, plus the foal's weight, are pressing backwards."

"Turn her around?" The girl's eyes bugged. "But it's just us and she weighs a ton."

"We don't have to pick her up," I said. "We just have to pivot her around her rear end. Sorry, but without it, we're not getting this foal out tonight, without drugs or help. I don't think she can wait much longer."

"But what if she slips down closer to the river?" The terror in the girl's eyes chilled me to the marrow, but there was nothing for it.

"We'll just have to try," I said, eyeing the rushing brown water down the hill, too close for comfort. I moved to Goldie's head, pulling off the rectal sleeve.

"Okay, what do I do?" Stacey bit her lip, hands poised.

"Grab her mane just behind her poll and I'll pull from the middle of her mane. Whatever you do, if she starts to get up, clear out. Got it?"

Stacey nodded and we wound our hands into the mare's mane, tried for purchase in the slithery grass, took a deep breath, and tugged.

The mare never moved.

Stacey looked at me, eyes wide, her face shining whiter than it'd already been in the faint light.

"All right, Stacey, lets try again, on the count of three," I yelled, over the pelting rain. "You'll need to pull as hard as you can, or we won't get her turned and this could seriously go to custard. We have no other choice."

Breathing hard, we again twined our fingers into the mare's mane, and on the count of three, gave it our all.

It seemed she wasn't going to move, then she shifted a fraction of an inch, and then she just slipped toward us, finishing with her nose facing straight down the hill. Goldie groaned and the girl ran to her head, speaking softly all the while.

I flicked a glance at the river, closer than before, and turned my face back to the horse.

"If she tries to get up, Stacey, you'll need to put your weight on her neck, like this." I ducked down behind the mare and placed my knees gently on the side of her neck, then slipped my fingers under the side of her halter. "Then you'll lift her nose up toward the sky. She can't get up that way."

With the girl's soft voice in my ears, I raced to the mare's back end, pulled on another inverted sleeve, lubed up and reached inside.

"Oh, thank you," I whispered. The foal had slid forward enough that I could easily get past that the sharp pelvic brim, up its curved neck, and a little further along to its jaw. Shaking now, praying with everything I had left in me, I gave a little tug on the side of its chin and held my breath.

The foal's neck started to straighten.

"Thank you, thank you, thank you," I whispered. "Stacey," I swallowed hard, barely able to speak for the sobs wrenching from my throat, "it's not a wry neck, so I think we might just get this baby out."

"I knew you could do it," she said, over Goldie's barrel. Her face shone wetly in a patch of moonlight. The wind still blew the clouds at top speed across the sky, but the rain was slowing.

I clamped my jaw shut again. The neck was bending, but

try as I might, the head wouldn't come around. I could get my fingers into the foal's mouth, but couldn't quite get it to come all the way. How, oh how, to make this work?

Then I remembered.

Thank you, Kit.

I slipped out again and pulled out one of the foaling ropes, by some freak chance still tucked in my shirt. After fashioning one end of the soft tether into a noose, I dipped it into the disinfectant water, then slid my arm in again and slipped the soft rope inside the foal's mouth and around its lower jaw. The first time, he let me pull his head around a little way, then he pushed it out with his tongue and moved his head back to its original position. I managed to pull it off twice more after that.

Grinding my teeth in frustration, I racked my brain.

"Stacey, I'm trying to get his head around. There's room, but the loop keeps slipping off."

There had to be a better way. How about a war bridle— over the foal's ears and through its mouth? I lengthened the noose and slipped it over the foal's ears. Biting my tongue between my teeth, I shoved the toes of my boots into the mud and pressed as hard as I could to slip a piece of the loop into its mouth. If only I could get the snare in place, I *could* pull that little nose around. I tried once, twice, then three times. Each time, either the slippery amniotic fluid or folds of amnion itself helped the rope slip off. I finally got it over both of the foal's ears *and* through its mouth, with no amnion in the way, just as its little jaws clamped down on my fingers.

"Ouch, you little beggar," I said, with a laugh, and the tension broke. "He's still alive, anyway."

"I just knew you'd do it."

"It's not out yet, but we're on track. I need your help again, Stacey."

After another stroke of the mare's neck, she scrambled back up to me.

"Can you keep gentle tension on this rope to make sure the snare stays in place?"

"I sure can," she said, her voice quavering, as the sky turned dark.

I turned my face upward and a few raindrops smacked me on the cheek.

Stacey took up the slack in the rope and the foals nose moved under my hand as I held the snare over the back of the slippery little ears. Its face came 'round until it was parallel with my arm and lined up with the birth canal.

"We're doing it," I said, jumping at a thunderclap, as the rain started to come in great swaths. "We may just be able to —ah!" I yelped at the flash of lightning, far too soon after the thunder, far too close. I glanced around the field. There were no tall structures or trees to take a lightning bolt.

I set my jaw and turned to face a dripping Stacey. "We have to make this happen right now," I said, my heart in my throat. "I need to take my arm out, but you need to keep this baby's nose here. Got it?"

"I'll hold it steady," she said.

Sliding my arm out, I grabbed the remaining foaling rope from the bucket and made a half hitch. I slid it up the nearest foot to just above the fetlock, made another hitch around its pastern, handed it to Stacey and did the same on the other foreleg with the opposite end of the rope.

"The foal's pretty big, but I think she should be able to push it out, now its head's in the right place," I shouted above the water sluicing down around us.

Together we pulled, but the foal wasn't budging. The mare was tired and the same forces of gravity that helped get the foal out of my way were now working against us.

"If only we could reach a post, but then, doh, I don't have

a pulley, either," I growled, then nearly leapt out of my skin at another thunderclap, closer at hand. We were working in a serious danger zone.

"Stacey, we need to stay down low, but we have to turn this mare around again so gravity can help us. I'm afraid to lose the foaling ropes, especially the head snare, but we have to risk it. I can put it back on if I need to."

Lightning flashed again. This time it came from all directions. Everything stood out in stark detail before me: the weakening mare, the little hooves just protruding, the terrified girl, the slashing rain, and then it was gone and I was working blind. My eyes saw white, and then nothing.

"Let's do it then," Stacey said.

I blinked, then lashed the foaling ropes together, then wrapped them around the foal's forelegs, by feel.

"You take her tail. I'll grab her bottom hind leg, then we'll pull her around down the hill. Pull toward her front feet, so we don't damage her tail."

On the count of three, we pulled. We strained and grunted, we tugged and swore, but she never moved. We tried again, and again, and again. I lost track of time. We finally collapsed at another flash of lightning, only a fraction of a second after a deafening thunderclap. I lifted my head and stared at Stacey.

Hot tears mixed with the freezing sleet on our cheeks as we crouched, defeated, pelted by the deluge that drowned out even the sound of the raging muddy water below.

My heart froze as the coppery scent of blood assailed my nostrils. Like something out of a horror film, a long arm, rivulets of red running off it, reached toward me.

13

I screamed and jumped to my feet, surreal visions of knives and bloody shower stalls before me, then spun around.

"KIT!" I shrieked.

"You ladies looked like you were having such a good time, thought I'd join you. Want a hand?"

I leapt for him and hugged him for a moment, then turned back to the mare.

"Please, help us get her turned. We should be able to get the foal out if we spin her around again," I said.

He was already onto it and grabbed the mare's lower hind leg. I took the upper, and with Stacey on her tail, on my count of three, we pulled the mare around until her tail was once again pointing downhill. Goldie seemed to rouse a bit and started to push. I dropped back down behind her, with another glance over my shoulder at the flooded river, and caught Kit's eye.

"You're far enough away from it, but you wouldn't want to fall in. It's blasted cold in there," he said, with the ghost of a smile and wiped at the dark stuff, it must've been blood, running down his face.

"How'd you get here? Are you okay?" I shook my head as I untangled the ropes and handed them to Stacey.

"Tell you later. Let's get this foal out, then I'll carry it up the hill into another field."

"Stacey, you hold this rope for me? I'll put some pressure on the head rope and we'll see if we can get this baby out."

Kit dipped his hand into the disinfectant and slipped his fingers inside Goldie and had a feel around. With one hand still inside, he looked up at me with a smile.

"You'll be fine now," Kit said, proud approval in his voice.

We pulled, steadily and slowly, and Goldie pushed. The foal inched toward me until its nose was out, then its whiskers twitched.

"I'll bet he just didn't want to come out into this rotten night and turned his head back on purpose." I chuckled.

"I wouldn't blame him," Kit said, with feeling.

Goldie gave a great push and the slippery dark foal slid out all at once, landing in my lap in a flood of amniotic fluid. Stacey and I stared at each other, then we both began laughing and crying at the same time.

"See?" She grabbed me around the shoulders. "Dr. Allen said you could do it, so I knew you'd make it happen, right, Dr. Allen?"

"Darn straight. Wouldn't have set her to the task if she couldn't," he said, and reached for my hand. "Well done, darlin', and you too, Stacey."

Unnoticed, the rapidly moving storm had dissipated, leaving in its wake flying clouds, the moon and bright stars, with a chill that cut the wet group to the bone.

"Let's get this baby to its—*his*—mama. It's a colt," I said, as Stacey and I bent to drag him toward his dam's head.

She whickered and lifted her head, then rolled onto her chest, in another gush of fluid.

"Look out guys," Kit said, "she's getting up."

I glanced up from the foal to see the mare's hindquarters heaving before me and jumped to my feet. The mare's legs quivered and one of her hind legs had a distinct wobble, but she stayed up and pivoted on her hind end to reach the colt. She worried at the foal with her lips, then started to lick him dry as he struggled up onto his chest and lay blinking at the rough wash. He let out a tiny, high whinny and the mare doubled her efforts. The little body swayed with each swipe of her big rough tongue until he shook his head and sneezed. She began nudging at the colt until he got his forelegs in front of him, like the back half of a tripod, and after a few attempts, made it to his feet. He stood, shaky, then with tentative steps, worked his way back to his dam's udder.

"Always amazes me how they do that... just out into the world, and they can get up and feed, just like that," I said, with a snap of my fingers.

The mare tucked up her belly and hunched her back as the colt found what he sought. I ducked down at the mare's shoulder to watch as the little guy's tongue slipped from his mouth and curled around one engorged nipple, licking, licking, until his lips sealed around the teat. He played with it for a few moments and then suddenly he was suckling. His mama's nuzzling of his rear end became more enthusiastic as he continued to drink.

"We take so many years to feed ourselves and run," Stacey mused, a big grin on her face.

"Look what I brought," Kit said, with a smile, as he handed me a bottle of iodine and a few small syringes.

"You're amazing," I said. "Iodine and tetanus antitoxin?"

He nodded.

"Stacey, was the mare vaccinated for tetanus?" I asked.

"Yes. She had a booster last month."

"Good, then he doesn't need an antitoxin. I hate giving

them unless I must," I said, as I filled a syringe with povidine iodine and soaked the colt's navel.

"Congratulations to you, all three, no four, of you," Kit said, looking around at Stacey, the mare and foal, and me. The mare ignored him and kept licking her foal.

"You look like a drowned, muddy rat," Kit said to me, as he wiped my face with a towel he magically produced from inside his shirt.

"Can't say much more for you, but at least we're not covered with blood. You okay?"

"It's a long way from my heart," he said.

"That lightning was *way* too close," Stacey said, with a shudder, as I rubbed my head and arms dry, then handed the towel to her.

"Sure was. When does your family return, Stacey?"

"They're coming back in the morning—and I can't wait." She laughed and wrinkled her brow. "Didn't think I'd ever say that. What teenager would?"

I laughed, remembering. I'd been more than happy to be left on my own, too.

An hour later, after a long walk around the top bridge, I was starting to defrost before the blast furnace comprising the diesel pickup's heater when Kit finally broke our companionable silence.

"You did well tonight, exceedingly well, Dr. Scott," Kit murmured, and took my hand.

"I was terrified," I shuddered, "but nothing died, the foal's up nursing, Stacey's not traumatized... and... I feel... complete." I filled my lungs and closed my eyes.

When I opened them again, Kit had pulled off the road. He was leaning back, a huge smile on his dial.

"I knew you could do it," he said. "You're not the same girl you were as a teenager. When I saw you standing up there... on the far bank... I thought my heart'd been wrenched out. I knew you could do it, but if something went wrong, I had to be there. I'd promised. I couldn't let you down," Kit said, wiping at the blood still seeping from a gash in his forehead.

"What's with all the blood?" I said, peering closer at the wound. It was more of an abrasion, surrounded by bruising.

"When you were up on that cliff, I heard you screech something about watching out, and turned to see that massive log heading my way. I dived and scraped my forehead on some rocks on the bottom." He squeezed my hand. "Thanks for the warning. I wouldn't have survived being hit by that log."

I climbed across the cab into his lap and wrapped my arms around him, tightly. Kit hugged me back.

"Thank you," he repeated.

"Any time. Just, next time, not so much drama, eh?"

"I'll plan on that." He shuddered.

"How did you get over to us, by the way? Stacey said you wouldn't find the bridge."

"I started walking—running, actually—through the brush along the river. It wasn't nice—blasted yellow star thistle everywhere. You'll be doing some surgery to get all the prickles out later this week," he said, with a twisted grin. "I eventually found a water pipe that ran from my side to the other."

I stared at him, aghast.

"You didn't," I whispered.

"I did. I probably have enough upper body strength to have swung across, but I'd been in that water once tonight already, and didn't reckon I wanted to try it again. I had the calving chains with me, so I tied a loop of chain around my bottom, padded it up with your towel, made another loop around the water pipe, tied that end, and prayed the knots would hold, then worked my way across, hand to hand. I made it, but I'm afraid my buns will never be the same."

"Real hero material," I said, shaking my head. "Think you

could do it again so we could film it? The headlines could read: 'Resident Risks Butt to Save Student and Horse'."

"Shucks, ma'am, nothin' to it," he drawled. "But really, you were a star tonight, and I'm so very, very proud of you."

"I appreciate that, but I'd never have gotten there without your help, Kit," I said, and proceeded to kiss him silly.

14

I reached down and stroked Aspen's neck as we rode through my fated glade.

"I thought you were afraid to get too involved, Kit."

He flicked at a fly on Mickey's neck and stared off into space for a few minutes before he spoke.

"After my disaster of a marriage, I swore I wouldn't get involved with anybody... but you kinda got under my skin," Kit said, and blasted me with his killer smile.

"I wasn't going to let anybody get under mine, either."

"You see," Kit said, "I was wondering... would you like to come to Christmas with my family? I'd like you to meet them."

I swallowed hard. This was what people called "significant".

"My mother's been wondering why I've been so happy lately—she worries about me." He gave a sheepish grin.

"Moms always worry about the kids," I said. "Mine does too."

"I was afraid to tell her about us, maybe afraid to jinx it, but I've told her now. They'll love you to pieces, Mom and Dad. Their ranch is up at Tahoe, just near the lake."

"It sounds wonderful," I said, my heart warming fit to burst.

"What about your family, though? Don't you have any other plans?"

"They're still away in New Zealand, so… it would've been a lonely Christmas, anyway. I was going to take more shifts over the holidays."

"I'd hate to take you away from all that extra work," he winked at me, "but I'll even leave the pager at the clinic again, just to sweeten the deal."

"I don't know," I frowned at him, a smile playing about my lips, "I might go into withdrawals without the work, but if you're offering carrots like a pager-less Kit, guess I'll have to go." I laughed.

"Road trip it is. Grateful Dead headin' down the highway. And Rudolph, too—jingle bells all the way. It'll be a wonderful Christmas," he said, as he reached across the gap between the two horses and took my hand.

KIT'S PICKUP eased off the highway into his family's driveway, snow crunching beneath the tires. He slowed as we approached a beautiful bay Thoroughbred with a matching foal at foot, standing behind the post and rail fence.

"She's my favorite jumper—the one I kept when everything got split up," he said, and tightened his jaw.

"Glad you still have her then," I said, taking a deep breath, and squeezed his fingers. "It'll all be fine."

"I know. Thank you for comin' home with me," he said, as we drove on toward the house.

"Glad you asked," I said, taking my eyes off the pair of

horses and looking forward through the windshield at what could only be Kit's family members, by their resemblance.

"The welcoming committee awaits." He smiled and shut off the engine, opened my door and handed me out into the freezing, dazzling sunshine, accented by the tang of the snow-drenched pines. His arm, warm over my shoulders, led me toward the group.

Any anxiety I might have had about meeting his family vanished into thin air as handshakes turned to hugs. Kit's sister, a female version of him, stood tall and leggy in designer clothing and manicured nails, while his father offered a hint of the distinguished gentleman Kit would become. His beautiful mother was kindness itself as she pulled us in the door, toward her warm, cinnamon-scented farmhouse-style kitchen.

CHRISTMAS MUSIC PLAYED in the background when we eventually migrated from the hand-hewn kitchen table toward the living room with our foaming mugs of fresh eggnog. The huge tree caught my attention, its fairy lights and ornaments glittering against long pine needles, but my mouth dropped open at the view of Lake Tahoe completely filling the longest wall of the room. Its blue-black expanse shimmered against the snow on the surrounding mountains.

"Who's dishing out the presents?" Kit's mother asked, settling herself on the sofa.

"My turn." Kit's sister smiled and began delivering packages around the room.

I hadn't expected anything, but had made gifts over the month since Kit had invited me. For his mother, a gardening apron; his sister, some padded hangers for her fashionable clothes; and for his pop, a big tin of the Danish Christmas cookies I'd grown up making with my family. Kit had already inhaled most of his cookies on the way up the mountain.

Soon there was a pile of gifts beside me. I stared at Kit over the top of it, my mouth open.

"What did you expect? You're part of the family, now. Enjoy it," he said, and leaned across to kiss me.

My face heated. I couldn't have been more pleased, as I picked up the first gaily wrapped package.

"A western shirt," Kit said, holding up his first present. "I haven't had a new one in years, thank you, Lena!"

"That forest green with chocolate is perfect on you, Kit," his sister said. "It looks designer, where did it come from?" She turned to me.

"It's a Lena original," I said.

"No, it can't be," she said, peering over her brother's shoulder at the label. "It is!"

"What does it say?" his mother asked.

"Made Expressly for Kit by Lena," she said.

Kit pulled it on and clicked the pearl snaps.

"It fits," he said, astonished. "They never fit... and it's actually long enough."

"Of course, it fits, I'm a professional. Just remind me to give back your ratty old denim work shirt that was falling apart at the seams."

"You didn't cut it apart, did you?" Kit said, horror written all over his face.

"Your precious shirt is safe," I said, squeezing his fingers. "I know how long it must've taken to get the fabric that soft."

"You got that right," he said, with a grin.

I glanced around, but everyone was absorbed elsewhere.

"Truth be told," I whispered, "you might not get it back."

He frowned, and I quirked my lips at him.

"What have you done with it?" His brows narrowed.

"Nothing, but it's awfully nice to sleep in… it's got your scent."

He peeked toward the rest of the family, then turned back to me, eyes glowing.

"Now that, I'd like to see," he said, in an undertone. "You can keep it, if that's why you need it." He chuckled.

The first present I opened was a beautiful copy of Robert Frost's *Birches*.

"That's for you, my dear," Kit's mother said, after I unwrapped it, "because you're a swinger of birches." Her eyes glowed as she gazed from me to her son and back again.

Everyone was happy with my homemade gifts and I was touched by the thought that had gone into their presents for me.

Kit disappeared for a moment, then returned to the room carrying a large, gaily decorated box. I glanced up at him with a smile and returned to reading about birches in the snow, my legs tucked up beneath me on the sofa.

All talk in the room ceased and I looked up to see Kit standing before me.

"This is for you." He gently handed the package to me and sat down. "It's breakable. Very."

Looking sideways at him, I slipped my feet to the floor and pulled the end of the silk ribbon to untie the bow, then pulled off the paper. Whatever it was, it'd been packed securely.

Kit cut the heavy tape securing the box with his pocket knife and I opened the flaps. Just inside was a small, leather-framed certificate from Worcester Royal Porcelain Company… a certificate for a numbered, limited edition.

I stared at Kit's soft smile and returned to the box. He helped me remove a bucketful of foam packing peanuts before some little dark ears peeked out, then the neck of a bay horse.

I carefully held its body while we tipped the rest of the packing into another box to expose a figurine.

But not just any figurine.

It was a porcelain mare and foal on a dark wood pedestal, modelled and painted in exquisite detail.

I shook my head at Kit, my mouth open.

"Your first foal," he said. "And what a foaling. I think you deserve it after that one."

"But Kit," I hissed beneath my breath, "you don't have the—"

"It's special, like you," he said. "It was modelled by the famous Doris Lidner and belonged to my grandfather. He left it to me and I want you to have it. When you look at it, remember that scared fifteen-year old… and what she's become. Never forget the lesson that foal taught you."

My eyes filled to overflowing, I carefully placed the statue back into its box and threw my arms around his neck.

"Why don't you two go for a walk before lunch?" Kit's mother suggested. "It's beautiful outside now, and it's meant to snow later."

"Shall we?" Kit offered his arm.

"Your family's wonderful, and your sister," I touched the lovely new golden silk scarf at my neck, "has exquisite taste."

"They think you're pretty special, too." Kit picked up some of the freshly fallen snow and blew on it until the tiny crystals melted. "I told my mom a bit about you," he grinned, "but I wouldn't tell my sister. She's been dying to see who's been keeping my attention all these months."

Shaking my head, I pulled Kit toward his truck to get his final present.

"You've already given me a gift," he protested, as he took it from my hands and began to unwrap it.

"Yeah, but this one's work related and... " I played with my fingernails, then looked up at him, "... it's sort of private... from when we started learning what mattered to each other. It didn't seem right to offer it in your parents' glittering living room."

He smiled and squeezed my hand, then his eyes widened at the new leather shoeing apron.

"Where did you find one with a tooled belt? Personalized?

On a student income? Lena, you truly shouldn't have," he said, frowning, before pleasure broke out all over his face. "It's even the same style as my old one!"

"Where do you think I got the pattern?"

He stared at me, jaw dropped.

"You made this, too?"

I nodded.

"I grew up working with fabric *and* leather."

"I'll wear it with pride." He kissed me. "Thank you... you do know me, don't you?"

"I'm beginning to," I said, with a smile.

"I have another gift for you, too." Kit said, as he pulled a small, slim package wrapped in Christmas paper from his pocket and took me in his arms. "I thought you might appreciate this." His eyes glinted like a summertime sea. "Another memento of our first dates."

As I unwrapped it, a diamond hoof knife sharpener peeked out from the tissue paper.

"Oh, thank you!" I smiled up at him and he pulled me closer, if it were possible.

"Look at the engraving," he whispered.

Lena Scott—DVM To Be

"And you understand me, too," I murmured.

"Don't say I never bought you diamonds," he said, with a laugh.

"That figurine is more special than any diamond." My face heated, as I looked down at the instrument in my hands, then away at the snow covering the trees beside us, and on toward the lake. "And I have thousands of glittering diamonds right here in the snow, and on the water."

He smiled and kissed me again.

"Oh," I said, as I remembered Jess's card.

"What's this?" Kit said, as I handed him the envelope, addressed to both of us.

"Christmas card from Jess. I haven't read it yet."

He opened it and laughed, then showed it to me.

Merry Xmas, you two.
    Remember to invite me to the wedding. All my love,
    Jess

We only barely twitched upon reading it.

The bay mare we'd seen from the driveway stood at the fence and whickered to Kit as we walked toward her. He opened the gate and motioned me through.

"Her name's Living Word," he said, nodding at the mare. "I call her Goody."

"She's beautiful," I whispered. "And what a gorgeous baby," I added, as the filly nosed me. I scratched the base of her withers and she preened.

"They are, aren't they? Lovely, like you," he said, wrapping one arm around me and looking away. "This filly will have to do us for a while."

"Pardon?"

"This filly will have to do us for a while," he repeated, his green eyes deep as the sea, as they gazed into mine.

My face tingled where he stroked it absently with the side of one finger and I shuddered.

"What *are* you on about?" I managed.

"About babies." He spoke slowly, deliberately. "Goody's baby will have to suffice for a while. We can't do real babies while you finish your veterinary degree, but we can talk about it. Ever fancied going to Sweden?"

"Professor Salandro?" I stared up at him and he nodded, his smile warm, as he pulled me in tight again.

"That's the best Christmas present, ever," I murmured

against his lips, my heart filled to bursting, when he finally let me breathe.

"And we owe it all to the horses," he said. "And now, every time I get out my apron—"

"—and every time I sharpen my hoof knife—" I echoed.

We froze, suspended in time, lost in each other's eyes.

"I don't know what it will take to stay together—" he said, his voice strong.

"—but it'll be worth every moment," I finished.

Kit looked down at me and I blinked, then shook my head in disbelief.

It was his pager-glow...

And Kit was giving it to me.

Life couldn't get any better.

The End

EPILOGUE

T*wo weeks later*
        Grateful Dead pounded away in Kit's living room while Kit made his morning rescue coffee and I studied my lecture notes at his kitchen table. I was meant to be studying, anyway, but when I glanced up from my notebook, a vet school faculty newsletter sitting halfway under a pile of research papers caught my eye.

I blinked at the headline on the first page and tugged the sheet carefully from beneath the stack, then stared at the print while a chill slid down my spine.

Fraternization with Students

"Ah, Kit? Have you read your faculty rag this week?" I stood, holding the missive carefully between my fingers, as if it might go off with a boom.

"No, why?" He didn't turn around as he poured water through the laden filter.

"I think you'll want to see it." I suspect my tone,

somewhere around a weak whisper, rather than my words, made him set the kettle down mid-pour.

"What is it?" His brow wrinkled as he put one arm around me and took the paper.

We read it together.

> "Fraternising with students by the staff of the school, including residents, will not be tolerated. Further residencies will not be granted to those pursuing relationships with students."

Kit didn't say anything.

He didn't need to. I tightened my arm around his waist and held him close against me.

He'd just sent off his application for the surgery residency he wanted here so badly.

Especially... after the letter from Professor Salandro last week, in which he'd said he was truly sorry, but he had given the surgery residency in Sweden to another applicant...

THANK YOU

Thank you for joining Lena and Kit in
Lena Takes a Foal.
Lena will be returning in other books in the series.

Enjoyed the story? Want to read more?
If you loved it, a short review on Bookbub, Goodreads and
your favorite eBook retailer would sure be appreciated.
I'd be grateful for your help in spreading the word!

Sign up for Lizzi's VIP Club to hear about new releases and
specials, plus get your free sampler gift here!

www.lizzitremayne/VIPFOAL

FIND BOOKS

Find eBooks at your favorite online retailer via buy links at
www.lizzitremayne.com

or

Purchase Softcover books:

from New Zealand and Australia,

My print books are available in standard (and some in large format)
print for your reading pleasure. Find bookstores stocking my
books at:

www.lizzitremayne.com/Booksellers

From Other Countries:

Print books are available in paperback from most online retailers and
in select bookstores around the world.

Find stockists at www.lizzitremayne.com/Booksellers

BOOKS BY THE AUTHOR

The Long Trails Series

Books 1-3: *The Long Trails Box Set: Historical Western Family Saga: Books 1-3*

Can an orphan, with only her Mustang and a Cossack sword, survive alone on the frontier?

From the deserts of Utah, through the gold mines of California, to the turbulent wilderness of Colonial New Zealand, Aleksandra rides, loves, and fights—with only her Cossack skills to keep her alive.

Book One: *A Long Trail Rolling*

Winner of the True West Magazine 2016 Best Western Romance, Winner Romance Writers of New Zealand: 2014 Pacific Hearts Award and 2015 Koru Award.

Hunted for her secrets. Hiding in plain sight. Can one woman blaze her own trail into untamed territory?

UTAH TERRITORY, 1860. Aleksandra has spent her whole life training for the inevitable. So, when a brutal Cossack tracks down and kills her father, she instinctively collects her pa's elixir and flees. But when she meets the mysterious Xavier at a nearby trading post, she wonders if she can win both his protection and his heart…

Disappointed when the man of her dreams leaves to join the Pony Express, Aleksandra dons a disguise to follow him into the dangerous frontier assignment. Hiding behind her martial arts skills and a male alias, she longs to tell the handsome Xavier the truth. But with the killer in pursuit, keeping up the ruse may be her only chance for survival…

Can Aleksandra save both her love and her family legacy from a relentless murderer?

Book Two: *The Hills of Gold Unchanging*

As the Civil War rages, secessionists menace California. The Confederates want the state and they'll stop at nothing to take it.

UTAH TERRITORY, 1860. On a wagon train headed West, Aleksandra makes an enemy of a gun-running Confederate when she fights her way out of his unwelcome embrace and Xavier's new friends realize he's heard too much to be allowed to live. Embroiled in the Confederate's fight to drag the new state from the Union and make it their own, can Aleks and Xavier survive? The secessionists mean business.

Book Three: *A Sea of Green Unfolding*

They set sail for the peace and calm of New Zealand, but they hadn't counted on murderers, mutineers, and a land war in paradise.

SAN FRANCISCO BAY AND NEW ZEALAND, 1863. Tragedy strikes in Aleksandra and Xavier's newly found paradise on their California Rancho but Von Tempsky's invitation draws them to a new life in peaceful New Zealand. They disembark into a turbulent wilderness—with the opening shots of the New Zealand Wars just being fired—straight at them.

Novella: **Somewhere Called Home**

Highlands to Waterloo—can love prevail over fate?

SCOTTISH HIGHLANDS, 1813.

Robert is disowned for refusing to become clan tacksman after his father and heads for the city, alone, to build a life for himself and his beloved Sofia. Sofia's waiting turns to despair when her mother buys safety during the clearance of their village—leaving Sofia at the mercy of the laird's degenerate son. Rob emerges from the hell of

Waterloo wanting only to see Sofia again... and his father. *To be released soon.*

The *Tatiana* Series

(with links to The Long Trails *series)*

Book One: **Tatiana I**

Stableman's daughter Tatiana rises to glamorous heights by her equestrienne abilities—but the tsar's glittering attention is not always gold.

MOSKVA, RUSSIA 1842. Tatiana and her husband Vladimir become pawns in the emperor's pursuit of a coveted secret weapon. While Tatiana and their infant son are placed under house arrest, Vladimir must recover the weapon or lose his wife and young son. With the odds mounting against them, can they find each other again—half a world away? *Coming soon!*

The Once Upon a Vet School Series

Drama and humor abound as Lena pursues her childhood dream of becoming an equine vet—and beyond—in this unique series of

six independent novella sequences:

~Junior Years~

After Lena hears she needs good grades to become a veterinarian, things start to get tricky. Even her pony doesn't get out unscathed. (Middle Grade) *USA 1972-1976*

~High School Days ~

When your high school counsellor says vet school's too hard for you and your HS sweetheart offers you a dream life of farming, writing, and babies, what do you do? Is vet school really the be-all, end-all? (Young Adult) *USA 1976-1979*

~College Nights

How can you have a life when you need an A in every class for four years to get into vet school... on top of 800 hours vet practice work? Something's got to give. (Young Adult and up) *USA 1980-1984*

~Vet School 24/7~

Now they're in, the pressure for grades is off and vet school social life is upon them... there's only the tsunami of 200 years of veterinary knowledge to pack into their heads. Can Lena and her friends stay afloat? (Young Adult and up) *USA 1984-1988*

~Practice Time~

Finally graduated, prima ballerinas of the university, Lena and her vet school classmates disperse to far-flung practices... and real life. What could possibly go wrong? Late nights on-call, mud, blood, and finally, a light at the end of the tunnel... unfortunately, it's only the penlight of a dictatorial vet technician in Lena's eyes after she passed out on the floor. (Women's Rural Fiction with Romantic Elements) *USA & New Zealand 1988-2012*

~Long in the Tooth~

When Lena suffers another catastrophic back injury in New Zealand, what's she to do to feed her family and keep the farm? She can't breathe around cats or birds and what good's an equine vet who can't hold up a horse's leg? Time for Lena to go back to school. Again. (Women's Rural Fiction with Romantic Elements) *New Zealand 2012- ...*

Currently Available Reads:
~Vet School 24/7~

Fifty Miles at a Breath

Horses bring them together and their future looks rosy—it's the present they can't handle.

When equine veterinary student Lena and veteran pilot Blake fall in love, vet school and the past intrude. Add in a long-distance relationship, and things get just plain hard. A grueling endurance race forces them to draw on their strengths and face their fears —together.

Lena Takes a Foal

She needs help... he needs to stay away...

Lena's got a problem—one that might prevent her from graduating. When her horse flips over and lands on her, it has to be the dashing resident, Kit, who finds her. Luckily, she's sworn off relationships after her last debacle and sea-green eyes and rugged good looks are the last things on her mind. Besides, to a veterinary school faculty, relationships between residents and students are like oil and water.

They just don't mix.

~Practice Time~

Greener Pastures Calling

A new country, a great job, and a good Kiwi bloke. Life couldn't be better.

Until it gets worse.

Newly emigrated to New Zealand, Lena wants a 'good Kiwi bloke', but they're elusive as their nocturnal namesake. Nigel's avoiding females, unless they're cows, horses, or his mother after his first marriage. Sparks fly when they meet—but not the first time, over the dirty instruments in a filthy cowshed. They seem to be made for each other, until Nigel remembers where he first saw her. And then the questions start.

Understanding Modern Vet Med for Owners

The new series of veterinary books for horse owners to let you use what vets know to keep your horses healthier and happier. *First volume due out soon!*

With Bluestocking Belles

Boxed sets of historical love stories from a host of bestselling authors.

Christmas 2018: ***Follow Your Star Home***

The Viking star ring is said to bring lovers together, no matter how far, no matter how hard.

In nine stories, covering more than half the world and a thousand years, our heroes and heroines put the legend to the test. Watch the star work its magic, as prodigals return home in the season of good will, uncertain of their welcome.

With Authors of Main Street

Boxed sets of *new* contemporary love stories from multiple bestselling authors, for a sweet romantic holiday treat.

Christmas 2017: *Christmas Babies on Main Street* *Nine stories from the bestselling Authors of Main Street!*

From the small hamlet of Eastport, to the gorgeous landscapes of New Zealand, to Main Street, USA, you'll find the Christmas spirit and warm love stories on every page.

Summer 2018: *Summer Romance on Main Street*

Seven stories from the Authors of Main Street!

Welcome to Main Street, where you'll find sweet summer romance and true love from small towns everywhere

Christmas 2018: *Christmas Wishes on Main Street*

Seven stories from the Authors of Main Street

Don't you love to hear everyone's Christmas wishes? Read our small town wishes and feel the love from Canada all the way through to New Zealand.

Sign up for Lizzi's VIP Reader Club to hear about new releases and specials, plus get your free sampler gift here!

www.lizzitremayne.com/VIPFoal

LIZZI TREMAYNE'S BOOKS
2019

COMING SOON!

WITH LOVE FROM
NEW ZEALAND, RUSSIA, SCOTLAND, AND U.S.A.

AUTHOR'S NOTES

On the off chance that you haven't figured it out by now, much of this story is based upon my life and times in veterinary school. Fortunately, I had no fear of foalings, and unfortunately at times, not enough fear of much else. Certainly not enough to keep me out of trouble.

My classmates certainly weren't as bad as Lena's, but I needed some external conflict in the story. There were many good people, and certainly many good horses, who made my life worth living throughout this time. You know who you are, and you have my heartfelt thanks.

One of these is Dr. Eric Davis, who's made an incredible difference to so many: animals, veterinary students, veterinarians, equid and other animal owners in under-served places from the Rez's through to South America... and just about anyone with whom he's come into contact. The multiple and myriad animals he's helped, who cannot speak for themselves, would thank him, and probably do. I'm sure he can hear them.

Today, Dr. Davis and his RVT wife Cindy Davis continue this with *R-Vets*. Their mission: to promote quality and affordable veterinary care in under-served rural areas in the USA and abroad, by providing veterinary students with practical experience and training in the medicine and surgery of horses and other animals. Further, in exposing students to the needs of these communities they encourage future veterinarians to choose rural service as a career.

Learn more about R-Vets at http://www.r-vets.org/

I hope you enjoy your foray into my world of veterinary fiction. If you liked it, help others find it by leaving reviews and comments where you purchased it, on Bookbub, Goodreads, and on my webpage. If you want to pass on a comment, please find me via my *Connect with Lizzi* page.

Warmest regards,

Lizzi Tremayne

RECIPE: JESS'S EASY SPAG BOL

Lena's favorite, especially when Jess is making it. This is a simple recipe and any student can put it togeth er in a few minutes while they're eating their breakfast. It'll be ready when you return home in the evening—just boil up some pasta or raviolis and Bob's your uncle! Tastes better than canned and costs less.

Makes 4-8 servings or dinner for yourself for most of the week.

Spag Bol

- **2-3 onions,** chopped roughly
- **4-8 (or more) cloves garlic,** minced
- **a pound or two ground beef,** if your budget lets you eat meat this week
- **oil for frying** onions, garlic, and meat
- **4 pounds very ripe tomatoes** from a roadside stand or your own plants, roughly chopped, or if

they're not available, use 3 x 28 ounce cans whole, crushed, or chopped tomatoes.

- **1-2 cups (175 ml) water**
- **1 tsp oregano**, chopped (fresh) or 1/2 tsp crumbled (dry) 1 tsp thyme, crumbled (fresh) or crumbled (dry)
- **1 tsp rosemary**, crushed (fresh) or crumbled (dry)
- **jalepeños, chopped, 2-6 slices**, depending upon heat and your tastes
- **pasta** as below
- **salt and freshly ground pepper** to taste, after all has cooked down.
- Use all spices and salt n pepper to your own taste. This is a good starting point.

Sauté onion in oil until golden. If using beef, either crumble in or make into meatballs before browning beside the onions. Place these into a crock pot or slow cooker set on high. Stir in tomatoes and the rest of the ingredients other than salt and pepper and simmer for the whole day, or overnight.

The Pasta

Your choice of wheaten, rice, or other pasta Place pasta into an oversized pot of salted water that's already at a rolling boil. Cook it, stirring just enough to keep it from sticking together and to the bottom, to your desired consistency.

If you want it to be lower GI, only cook it 'al dente', or so it 'has teeth', meaning on the light side, less than about 5-7 minutes, depending on many factors, including your altitude. Look it up. Pasta should still be firm, but taste cooked.

If you don't care about glycemic indices, or like very soft pasta, cook a little longer.

Drain the pasta and serve it at the table with the sauce and a big ladle and let everyone dig in. A grater and a block of parmesan cheese is a nice addition if your student budget will let you go there... or cheddar or Monterey Jack if you prefer.

Enjoy!

(If you want to get all serious about it, though, here's a "real" Italian Spag Bol recipe: http://bit.ly/2yLrh0h)

ABOUT THE AUTHOR

Lizzi grew up riding wild in the Santa Cruz Mountain redwoods, became an equine veterinarian at UC Davis School of Veterinary Medicine and practiced in the Gold and Pony Express Country of California before emigrating to New Zealand. She has two wonderful boys, a grandbaby, and an awesome partner in that sea of green. When she's not writing, she's swinging a rapier or shooting a bow in medieval garb, riding or driving a carriage, playing in the garden on her hobby farm, singing, cooking, or looking into a horse's mouth in her equine veterinary dental practice. She is multiply published and awarded in special interest magazines and veterinary periodicals.

With this debut novel, she was Finalist 2013 RWNZ Great Beginnings, Winner 2014 RWNZ Pacific Hearts Award for the unpublished full manuscript, Winner 2015 RWNZ Koru Award for Best First Novel and third in Koru Long Novel, and Finalist 2015 Best Indie Book Award.

CONNECT WITH LIZZI

I'm looking forward to hearing from you!

Join conversations and find story excerpts, buy links, and more here:

www.lizzitremayne.com/VIPFoal
www.lizzitremayne.com
www.horseandvetbooks.com
www.bookandmainbites.com/LizziTremayne/
www.bookbub.com/profile/lizzi-tremayne/
www.facebook.com/lizzitremayneauthor/
www.instagram.com/lizzitremayne/
www.twitter.com/LizziTremayne/
www.youtube.com/user/lizzikiwi/
www.goodreads.com/LizziTremayne/
https://nz.pinterest.com/lizzitremayne/

ACKNOWLEDGMENTS

My forever thanks to:

~Eric Thompson. Thank you from the bottom of my heart for making my life easier while I was at university. That final year, when I didn't have to work because you and Mum supported me, was a true gift. Even afterwards: the truck at graduation, Levi Ride & Tie, and the trip to rescue me (with horse, no less) from Southern Cal. I'll never forget. You've always been there for me, even after you and Mum split. Every time I glance around my office, bright and sunny because there are two skylights where there were none, I always think of you and remember the fun days. Thank you so much, for all.

~Matthew, for everything, not least your awesome ideas about this finale, my pain-free wrists, 22-inch touch screens, and far too many other things to even begin to list. xx

~beta readers extraordinaire: Jude Knight, Matthew Tremayne, Shelagh Merlin, E. Ayers, Kate Le Petit, Greta Gordon, and

Kirsten Davidson, and to my readers: I appreciate your wonderful comments and questions. Keep 'em coming! xx

~Emily Ashton and the Portmeirion Group, for their kind permission to use my own image of the Royal Worcester Porcelain Company's Prince's Grace and Foal figurine on the original cover of this story.

~Doris Lidner, modeller of Prince's Grace and Foal. My heartfelt appreciation for the exquisite modelling and painting of her many, many figurines of horses and dogs, with their people.

~Jeff Ketzler, president of The Dehner Company, Inc., for his permission to use the name of their boots in this story. I truly waited two decades for a pair. Like Lena, I didn't want my boot cut off, either.

—the many others who have helped in so many other ways, including your everyday encouragement to finish this story and get it out! Thank you all. I couldn't have done it alone.

xx

Lizzi

EXCERPT FROM A LONG TRAIL ROLLING

A*pril 1860, Echo Canyon, Utah Territory, U.S.A.*

SHE SMELLED BLOOD. Its metallic tang assailed her senses before it was overshadowed by the stench of death. Stepping back to scan the sheer wall of the bluff rising before her, her breath caught in her throat and a sob escaped.

Finally, she'd found him.

A scuffed black boot and fur coat showed through the snow, his body wedged into the bottom of a crevice three feet above her head. She looked up to the top of the cliff, from which he must have fallen, but saw no one.

Finding handholds where there were none, Aleksandra Lekarski scrambled up the wall as her heart constricted in her chest. She tugged her father's cold, stiff body free and down onto level ground, giving thanks he'd been out of reach of the wolves whose tracks abounded in the snow where she now stood. Her world blurred as she dropped to her knees and cradled his lifeless head in her lap, rocking him. Ceaseless tears flowed down her doeskin tunic.

With a numbing pain in her mind, she ran shaking hands over him, seeking answers. What could have made an experienced trapper like Krzysztof Lekarski fall off a bluff and succumb to a death more suited to a greenhorn?

This couldn't really be happening.

Just seven days ago, he'd kissed her goodbye with glowing eyes.

'Keep the fire going in the smokehouse this time, will you, Aleks?'

'Of course, Papa, my promise. Be back soon, I'll miss you.'

'I'll return before you've missed me, then we'll go sell last winter's furs at the trading post.'

We'll never go to town together again.

Aleksandra sat back on her heels and gripped her swimming head in her hands, fingers pulling her hair until it hurt, then whimpered and returned her attention to her papa.

She shrank from what was left of his eyes... and was glad he'd been in the narrow gap, too small for large predators. Beetles had been there, or some rodent, maybe even a hawk. The scent of decay was a sharp contrast to the clean bite of fresh snow. Trying not to breathe through her nose, she swallowed hard, stomach rolling.

Aleksandra's hands froze as hard-crusted blood met her fingertips. Her heart stopped altogether at the sight of the inch-long, bloodied cut in his buckskin jerkin, repeating into his chest wall. She turned him over. A laceration of the same size exited the soft leather covering his back.

Papa hadn't simply fallen off the bluff. Nothing but a sword made such a wound.

Aleksandra's ears began to ring, her world narrowing to a small gap, as she fought the rising panic.

It couldn't be…Vladimir couldn't *have found us. Not over two decades, two continents and the Atlantic Ocean.*

The ground swayed as she hunched over her father's still form. Squeezing her eyes shut to stop the motion, she recalled the words Papa had endlessly repeated, so she would always remember:

'He *will* seek us out. Vladimir will come for the secret and we must be prepared to keep it from him—at all costs —always.'

But what a cost.

Despite her entire being screaming to fall apart for the loss of her only remaining family, years of Papa's training to protect their secret stopped her in her tracks. Struggling to draw air into her lungs, she looked around the bottom of the cliff. Her clearing vision now showed more wolf sign: scrapings on the wall below his body and white snow darkened by blood beside stinking yellow patches.

Leaving his body here, knowing the scavengers would return, would be the hardest thing she'd ever done—but Aleksandra knew what her papa would have required of her.

Heart sinking, she slumped to the forest floor beside him and took a deep breath of the wind whistling cold up the valley. Closing her eyes, she touched her lips to the top of his head. With shaking hands and tears flowing anew, Aleksandra lifted the leather thong of the beaded *Shoshone* medicine bag from about his neck and pulled the signet ring from his finger. Kissing her papa once more, she covered him with dead leaves and snow, beseeching the forest spirits to care for him with love, if she couldn't return.

She rose and turned to leave, but through the brain-fogging misery, she remembered to check for the tools of Papa's trade. The trapper's sword scabbard was empty and his rifle missing. The firearm was nearby, half covered by a snowy branch, but even after searching for precious minutes, his *shashka* was nowhere to be found. With a twinge of regret, she gave up seeking her father's Cossack sword. She shouldered the rifle and stared back at the man she loved beyond life, her heart in a vise, with a promise and a prayer for his soul. Tears dried cold and tight on her face as she stood gazing past the putrefying corpse to the heart of her papa. She returned once more to brush back the frozen leaves and kiss him goodbye.

Her eyes scanned the aspen glade in the brilliant morning light. No one watched. With the silence and speed of the *kwahaten*, the antelope, her name with the *Shoshone* people who had welcomed her family into their own, she ran for her pony.

'It's you and me now, Dzień,' she choked out as she untied him and slung the rifle on her back. Vaulting on as he struck off into a lope, they flew back toward the cabin, the Indian pony seeming to sense the urgency and single-mindedness of his mistress. Slowing him to a stealthy walk as they neared the cabin, she slid from Dzień's back, signaling him to wait. She crept closer to the cabin. Before its open door, papers lay scattered beneath a light dusting of snow, fluttering in the chill breeze. The open barn doors slowly swung back and forth.

By now Papa's stallion should have been tearing up the stable and his field, but Rogan was gone. She waited, straining every muscle for any sound, but only silence met her ears, save the creaking hinges. She tiptoed around the perimeter of the yard in soft deerskin moccasins, keeping to the tree shadows as she'd done with her *Shoshone* friends in play. Hidden in shadow, Aleksandra stole to the window at the back of the cabin and peered in.

Her breath caught at the destruction. An intruder had turned the cabin upside down and must have set-to the place with a sword. The white softness of sliced feather-tick mattresses covered every surface and bedclothes were ribboned and strewn over the floorboards, but there was no movement.

She eased the door open and slid inside, hand on the hilt of her own *shashka*.

The doors of the oak secretary, Krzysztof's gift to Aleksandra's mother just before her death two winters ago, lay open. She nearly cried to see its drawers flung helter-skelter and papers scattered.

Utensils danced amongst broken crockery and cast iron pans. In some dim recess of her mind, she noticed the *zakwas* and sourdough pots still stood on their shelf behind the cook stove, high above the chaos.

She broke into a sweat at the sight of the stove lids lying in deep, black grooves in the wooden floor of the cabin. Lids hot enough to burn themselves into the cedar planks meant she'd narrowly missed the visit of the intruder when she left the cabin to find her pa.

She froze. Nothing of value seemed to be missing. This was only a search. Her heart sank further at the sight of the sun-bleached muslin dress on its peg in the corner by her bed, doubtless informing the unwelcome visitor, by now almost certainly the Russian Vladimir, that someone besides Krzysztof lived here.

Aleksandra climbed onto the table and peered up into the eaves. Papa's velvet-lined boxes were still in their places. She lifted the lids and nearly smiled, then hopped down and slipped out the door. Skirting the yard again, she noiselessly opened the back door of the barn and peeked in. The summer smell of new hay assailed her nostrils as she entered and surveyed the damage. The trespasser had been busy here too.

Harnesses and building tools were scattered about the dirt floor, the contents of the feed room and hay pile scattered.

Well, that accounts for the scent.

The buckboard wagon and dogcart were still there, but the gate rails of Rogan's loosebox lay where they'd been dropped. The manure in the stall was dry, several days old.

She glanced around the darkened corners of the barn and the yard outside once more before returning to squeeze her hand into the secret cache behind the colt's feed bin. As her fingers chilled at the touch of the dozen or so frigid glass vials and the box next to it, her lips twisted into a bittersweet smile. For the first time in days, the leaden melancholy lifted from her shoulders, if only a little. Despite the destruction, Vladimir had missed what he came for.

What now? Aleksandra ruminated, shaking her head, then took a great lungful of air.

Dzień trotted up at her whistle and she resolutely wiped her tears onto his mane, then hugged him around the neck with the hint of a smile.

'Papa's secret is safe, Dzień. We can bring him home,' she murmured, pressing her face into his furry neck. Reaching around, he nuzzled her derriere in reply and Aleksandra twisted to kiss him on his white star. She pulled the bedroll and bags from her saddle, then led him to the travois just inside the barn. She adjusted the two long poles, bound together with woven rawhide strips, then covered the widest part of the litter with a buffalo rug. Her papa's conveyance was complete.

On the long walk back to the bluff, she thought of her father's loving touch, his constant presence in her life, his sweet smile, his twinkling eyes. She would have them no more. Spiraling downward again, the thought of drowning in the emptiness was almost welcome, but she gritted her teeth and mentally shook herself. The focus was now on survival. Aleksandra suspected Vladimir didn't know the exact nature of what he sought, but nonetheless, he would return. She needed to be ready. Better yet, gone.

Aleksandra didn't fool herself. Her father, a survivor of Austro-Hungarian-occupied Poland, spent countless hours teaching his children self-defense. Unfortunately, Aleksandra's skills with a *shashka* were a fraction of those of her papa's... and even less than those of *his* own teacher, Vladimir. The Russian was, according to Papa, unsurpassed with the short Russian Cossack sword.

'You're a good swordsman, Aleks, but your impetuosity gets you into trouble,' Papa always said, shaking his head as he disarmed her, yet again. The last time, he'd added: '...whether you're sparring at *shashkas* or trying to knit for the memory of your mama, God rest her soul, who tried to reconcile you to your femaleness.'

Aleksandra grinned through her tears. Knitting that always ended up as a wad of uneven and dropped stitches—inevitably thrown in fit of temper onto a set of antlers high upon the sitting room wall.

ROUNDING the bottom of the bluff, Dzień picked up his head and pricked his ears, sniffing the breeze, then headed for the pile of leaves covering Krzysztof. He stopped dead six feet away.

Aleksandra gave him a pat on the neck and tried to smile, but failed. She left the pony's head to adjust the travois. Breathing deeply through flared nostrils, Dzień stepped towards Krzysztof. He shook his mane, then nuzzled the lifeless body, knocking off the leaves as he checked the man's full length. Dzień tapped him with a front hoof, then snorted and turned away, showing the whites of his eyes as he stared at the motionless man from the corner of one eye. Aleksandra's gut wrenched.

Blood pounded in her head as she struggled to drag Krzysztof's six-foot frame onto the makeshift stretcher. Dzień craned his neck around to watch, his muzzle and the skin about his eyes tensed and strained.

The pony responded to Aleksandra's gentle urging and took Krzysztof home one last time. She would bury him with his beloved wife and sons in their overpopulated graveyard, then determine how to elude Vladimir and survive.

'Can't protect our secret if you're dead, *moje drogie córki.*' Papa's words came back to her, in his thickly accented but precise English.

"*My darling daughter.*" Gulping, she clutched her father's medicine bag and choked back more tears, realizing she'd never hear those words again.

Sign up for Lizzi's VIP Readers Club to hear about new releases and specials, plus get your free sampler gift at www.lizzitremayne/VIPFOAL

EXCERPT FROM TATIANA

M *id-1842 Moskva, Russia*

BY THE TIME I was fifteen, and Vladimir sixteen, we were inseparable. No longer did he clean stalls as punishment, but to help me before his Training School classes began. This gave us more time to fit ourselves and prepare our combined *džigitovka* performances. We had been selected as part of the team to perform for the Tsar on his next visit to Moskva from St. Petersburg.

The tsar's creepy messenger, who came to our door with increasing regularity for no seemingly good reason, had delivered the invitation for our group to give the performance. His terse smile showed through the lace curtains as he stood before the door. I managed to talk Papa into answering it, claiming I couldn't leave my cooking pot.

The messenger, whose name I never asked, but he told me anyway, was Sambor Andropov. Due to his frequent visits, I had taken to ignoring anyone knocking on the door when I

204 | LIZZI TREMAYNE

was in the house alone. His mere eyes on me made my skin crawl, and I felt I was being undressed before his eyes. Although a servant of the tsar could not be ignored without serious repercussion, if he didn't know I was there, all would be well. If the message was important, he would return, or Mrs. Bagrov would get the door if she was in.

I had the grace to be embarrassed when I realized he had carried such a special invitation to our door after I had avoided him. It was just that men and boys in Papa stableyard never looked at me like that, so perhaps I was being overly sensitive. I vowed to be kinder to him when I saw him next. He was, after all, just doing the tsar's bidding.

After this missive, our training intensified. We only had a month to prepare our troop for our presentation before Tsar Nicholas and his Empress Alexsandra Feodorovna.

There were eleven men in our group, plus me. We were drawn from the wider area around Moskva, but bragging aside, Vladimir and I were the stars of the show.

We had a joint act, with a quadrangle, jumping and shashka work, but our own little act was the best one. It began with Vladimir and I standing in Sarda's saddle, with me just behind him, one hand in the air, waving at the audience. We would then do a lift, ending up with my standing upon Vladimir's shoulders—at a full gallop.

It was a truly tricky maneuver, and one that few ever attempted. We lived, ate and breathed *džigitovka*. In any spare time, we worked out together— running, press-ups, sit-ups— we needed all the strength we could muster, and on the day of the performance for the Tsar Nicholas and Tsarina Alexandra Feodorovna, we triumphed.

During our bows to their Excellencies, the Empress Alexandra Feodorovna beckoned us closer.

"Your skills," she said, "for such young people are to be rewarded. I should like to see you both again." She paused for a moment. "Perhaps," she glanced at the tsar, who lifted an eyebrow at her, and then turned back to us, "you would like to attend the ball at the Kremlin tomorrow night?"

I swallowed hard.

"We should be honored, your Excellencies," Vladimir said, his voice smooth.

"We will see you there." The tsarina nodded and turned back toward her husband, dismissing us.

I curtsied as gracefully as I could, holding a pair of reins and wearing jodhpurs and boots, lacking the essential skirts. Vladimir drew me to my feet and escorted me away.

"A ball at the Kremlin?" I blinked and took a deep breath. "However will I find a ball dress before tomorrow night?"

"You have none?" He looked at me, jaw dropped.

I peered from beneath my brows. "How many balls have I attended since we met?"

He stared at me. "Well…"

"Exactly. I attended the end of year cadets ball with you last year, but that dress will hardly be suitable for an audience," I indicated my breeches and boots, "other than this, of course, with the tsar and tsarina. It's easy for you. You simply need your Training School dress uniform."

"Sisters. Yes, that's it." He spun to face me. "Olga and Sonja will have a dress to fit you."

My jaw dropped. His sisters were elegant young ladies. I'd been introduced to them before, but they hadn't seemed impressed by the stable girl performing with their brother. "But they live a full day's ride away. I'd never be able to ride there and return and still take care of my stable duties."

"I'll go. I can get one of the other lads to do my work for me, if your father permits."

"I permit," he said, walking up in time to hear the end of the conversation.

"Thank you, sir. I have three sisters, most of them close in size to Tatiana. With your permission, I will leave as soon as I cool out my horse."

"We'll take care of that and inform the headmaster. Well done, both of you. Your performance was without equal," he said, taking the reins of Vladimir's horse and leading him back toward the barn.

"Papa," I said, and he turned. I reached out for Sarda's reins. "Thank you, for all you've done for me, for us." I glanced at Vladimir's retreating back.

He handed them to me and hugged me, his eyes glistening with unshed tears. "You have made me so proud, both you and Vladimir. What a team you make."

"We could've never done it without you."

"Soon he will be finished here and must enter the tsar's army." He took back Sarda's reins and together we began walking the sweating horses. "Have you considered what you will do then?" His eyes looked at me—through me—and I shuddered, then swallowed and looked at the floor.

"I honestly do not know, Papa."

"A life of horses is hard for a man, much less a woman, and I won't be around forever."

My eyes snapped up to his. "What?" For the first time, I saw his weathered visage, the grayness of his skin at the edges, and my stomach clenched. "Papa, are you ill?"

He took a deep breath. "I'm not sure, but my heart, it does funny things sometimes. Not badly, but it's enough to give me pause—to question and to ensure you are provided for."

The walls of the Kremlin swayed around me. Papa was my rock, although I'd been increasingly leaning on Vladimir as we had become close friends, and now, it seems, something more.

"Have you been to a doctor, Papa?" Knowing he hadn't.

"No, but there is little they could do."

"You don't know that…"

"Trust me, I know. Anyway, *princessa*, you will be going to the ball and dancing the night away on the arm of your prince.

"Will you becoming?"

"The invitation was only for the two of you, but I will be awaiting your return with bated breath." I offered the horse a few sips of water from a bucket then pulled Sarda away and we resumed our walk.

"This will be my first ball without you, Papa..." I searched his face, seeking to know the extent of his sickness, but nothing showed.

"My *solnishko* has grown up." New tears in his eyes threatened to fall. "You will be the loveliest woman there."

Woman.

I'd never thought of myself as that...it would take some time to sink in.

Due out soon! Look for it!

Sign up for Lizzi's VIP Club to hear about new releases and specials, plus get your free sampler gift at
www.lizzitremayne/VIP

Thank you for reading.
I hope you enjoyed Lena Takes a Foal!
·
Sign up for Lizzi's VIP Readers Club to hear about new releases and specials, plus get your free sampler gift at

www.lizzitremayne/VIPFoal

www.ingramcontent.com/pod-product-compliance
Lightning Source LLC
Chambersburg PA
CBHW020642260626
47157CB00008B/2871